RETURN OF THE WITCH

WITCHES OF KEATING HOLLOW
BOOK FOURTEEN

DEANNA CHASE

Bayou Moon Press, LLC

www.deannachase.com

Printed in the United States of America

ABOUT THIS BOOK

Three years ago, budding rockstar Levi Kelley broke up with the love of his life. He knew a long-distance relationship would be hard, but he didn't know it would break him. As a teen, he'd been thrown out then exploited for his unusual witch abilities, so the one thing he couldn't handle was the crushing feeling of abandonment. And that's exactly how he felt after one too many missed connections, miscommunications, and disappointments. There wasn't anything to do but go their separate ways. But now, after two years of touring the world, Levi is finally coming home to Keating Hollow... and his one love, Silas Ansell.

Air witch Silas Ansell has always wanted two things: a successful acting career and Levi Kelley. At one time, he'd had both. Then he lost Levi, and his acting career went sideways when his paranormal drama was canceled. Now he's coming home, determined to get both back. But what will he do if he has to choose between the two... again? Is love enough or will he find a way to get everything he's ever wanted?

CHAPTER 1

*L*evi Kelley clutched the script in his hand and wondered if it was too late to back out of his contract. Just what in the hell had he been thinking when he'd signed on to star in a movie with his ex? He was a musician, not an actor.

Sitting in his dressing room, he picked up his phone and dialed his agent.

Dawson picked up on the first ring. "Levi. Is everything okay? How's the first day going?"

"Terrible. You need to get me out of this."

There was silence. Not even the sound of office din in the background.

"Dawson?" Levi asked. "Are you there?"

"I'm here. What happened?"

"I just saw Silas, and I really don't think I'm going to be able to do this." Levi leaned back in his chair and closed his eyes, trying to block out the gut-wrenching ache that had materialized twenty minutes ago when he'd run into his ex. He'd thought he was over Silas Ansell. He'd forced himself to watch all of Silas's shows and movies just to prove that he could. In the two years since they'd broken up, Levi hadn't seen him in person or even called him. They'd broken up for a reason.

A very good one.

And now? Levi was going to be forced to spend every day of the next three months with Silas, pretending they were falling in love.

"We talked about this," Dawson said carefully. "I thought you said you were fine with working with Silas. That enough time had passed and you were ready to be friendly with him at least."

Yeah. That's what Levi had thought. He'd just finished his tour and was on an emotional high when the offer to star in the movie had come out of the blue. Normally, he wouldn't have considered doing any movie. Acting wasn't something he'd ever seriously considered. But the movie was written by Miranda Moon and Cameron Copeland, two residents of Keating Hollow, and it starred his ex, Silas Ansell. He'd instantly said yes, knowing that opportunities like that didn't come around a second time.

When Dawson had questioned him, asking if he'd really considered what it would mean to star opposite his ex, Levi had dug in. He wasn't going to let Silas ruin this chance for him. He'd already made far too many sacrifices for the man in the years they'd been together. This time, Levi was doing something for himself. Silas be damned.

But now, seeing him… Levi had severely underestimated how hard it would be to just be around Silas.

"Levi?" Dawson asked. "Are you still with me?"

"Yeah."

"I can try to get you out of this, but to be honest, it'll be very messy. The studio is going to be very unhappy and will likely threaten lawsuits. Not to mention the tabloids and paparazzi will be in a frenzy."

Levi let out an exaggerated sigh. "This is your way of telling me I've made my bed and now it's time to suck it up and lie in it, right?"

"Sort of. But I work for you, so if you want me to test the waters, I will."

A knock sounded on his door. "Levi? We're ready for you."

Levi's gut churned with anxiety, but he shook his head, even though Dawson couldn't see him, and said, "No. You're right. If I back out now, the gossip rags will never let this go. I'll... I don't know. Figure it out, I guess."

"Call me if you need me," Dawson said.

"I will. Thanks." Levi ended the call, went into his bathroom and splashed water on his face, and then made his way out of his trailer and into the barn where the rest of the cast was settling in for the first table read.

Silas took a seat across from him, and Levi looked at everyone but Silas. Seeing his dark expressive eyes and not knowing what was going on behind his guarded expression was too much.

Levi needed to get out of his head. He needed to focus on the script.

"Welcome everyone," said a man dressed smartly in blue trousers and a vest to match. He straightened his blue-and-purple-striped tie and cleared his throat. "I'm Marcus Maloney, the director of this film. Thank you all for being here. We couldn't be more excited to be filming with you. Now, before we start, you should know we made some changes to the script. The basic idea is still the same, but Miranda and Cameron have changed the backstories of the two protagonists and added some more insight as to why our two heroes are so reluctant to trust each other. We are all of the opinion that this makes the script stronger, and we can't wait to dive in. Are you ready?"

There were nods and murmurs of agreement.

Levi opened the new script that had been laid in front of him and scanned the first page. It was a scene starring River Ramon—Levi's character—and his mother, who appeared to be his manager. They're having an argument about the direction of River's career. They argue about him doing a commercial, and then River storms out and finds himself running into Ezra Jackson, Silas's character.

"Hey! Watch it," Silas read from the script.

"Sorry." Levi said his line, having to look at Silas now that they were getting into it.

The script had River steadying Ezra and the two of them sharing a quiet moment as they took each other in.

Everyone at the table was silent as Levi and Silas seemed to act that moment out from their respective chairs. Their gazes held, and years of unspoken words seemed to pass between them.

"Wow," the actress who was playing Levi's mom said, so quietly that Levi barely heard her.

"I think we all agree. Save some of that for the camera, okay, boys?" Marcus said.

"Oh, this is going to be good," a gorgeous blonde said from a few seats away.

Silas cleared his throat and stared down at his script.

Levi would've given anything to know exactly what his ex was thinking in that moment. Because all Levi wanted to do was grab Silas by the wrist, drag him back to his dressing room and... do what? Kiss the hell out of him? Demand answers? An apology? He had no idea, but every cell in his body screamed that he needed to get Silas alone.

And that's why, when they were finally done with the table read and Marcus told them all they were done for the day, Levi stood and walked out without a word to anyone.

Just when Levi had reached his Jeep Wrangler, his spirit magic kicked in and he felt the energy of someone behind him.

Silas.

Levi froze with his hand on the door handle. He was a spirit witch and could sense when people were near. He didn't always know who the person was, but he'd know his ex's energy anywhere.

"Can we talk for a minute?" Silas asked.

No, Levi thought. But then he straightened his shoulders and turned around, meeting Silas's still-guarded expression. "What's there to talk about?" he asked.

"I..." Silas cleared his throat. "I just wanted to say that it's good to see you."

Levi wasn't expecting that and felt a small tug at his heart. Dammit. He needed to shut that down. How was he going to work with Silas if he couldn't get past his feelings for him? Not knowing how to respond, he just muttered, "Okay."

Frustration finally broke through in Silas's expression, and Levi knew his response had irritated him. But Silas quickly schooled his features. "I just wanted to congratulate you on the role." He let out a nervous chuckle. "I didn't even know you wanted to pursue acting."

"I didn't," Levi said automatically. It was the truth after all. "Or rather, I didn't know either. But when the offer came in, I decided it was an opportunity that I couldn't refuse. And now here we are. For better or worse, I guess."

Silas shoved his hands into his jean pockets and lifted his

shoulders as he tilted his head slightly to the side, studying Levi. "So you didn't sign on because of me?" His tone conveyed sarcasm, but Levi knew better. Silas genuinely wanted to know if Levi was there for him.

"No, Si, I didn't pursue a movie just to be close to you. This is for me, for my career. Is that so hard to believe?"

"No." Silas shook his head, his expression serious again. "Of course not. I was just..." He shrugged. "I don't know what to think. You being here was a huge surprise. Not what I expected. It just threw me, is all."

"Sure." Levi needed to exit this awkward conversation ASAP. "I'm sure you'll get used to it." He opened the Jeep door, but Silas's hand on his shoulder stopped him. He turned around to look at Silas again. "What is it?"

Silas's voice was low and full of emotion when he spoke. "I wanted to say how sorry I am about what happened between us."

"Yeah, I know you are," Levi said, swallowing the lump in his throat. Even though they'd broken up, Levi had never questioned whether Silas loved him or not. He had. He just hadn't loved him enough to give him what he needed. "But that's all in the past, right?"

"Sure." Silas nodded. "I just wanted you to know. And I was hoping maybe we could be... friends?"

"Friends?" Levi parroted, not at all sure how that would work. But he was the one who'd made the choice for them to work on a romantic movie together. If they couldn't at least be friends, it would never work.

"Yeah, you know, what we were before we started dating. It worked then. It could work now," Silas said.

Levi let out a small chuckle. "Si, I hate to tell you this, but we were never *just* friends." Then he shrugged and said, "Sure.

We can be friends. But right now I have to get home. Hope is cooking dinner."

Silas nodded and held out his hand. "Shake on it?"

Levi grabbed his ex's hand and as soon as they touched, a ripple of electricity tingled up his arm, making gooseflesh pop out over his skin as a shiver worked its way through his body.

Silas sucked in a sharp breath, indicating that he'd felt it too. Before Levi could let go, Silas tugged gently on his hand and then pulled him into a tight hug and whispered, "I'm so proud of you, Levi. I'm very sorry I wasn't able to share the last two years with you."

Then he let go and strode away, leaving Levi gaping after him.

CHAPTER 2

From the moment Silas had learned that Levi was starring in his movie, he'd been in a state of shock, completely unable to comprehend how it had happened.

Intellectually, he knew of course. The other costar, Will Weeks, had been seriously injured in a car crash and had dropped out at the last minute. Since everything was set up and ready to go with filming, casting had scrambled to find not just a suitable actor, but one who could sing as well. The main protagonist was a rock star, after all. Never in a million years would Silas have imagined they'd give the role to Levi Kelley.

Though he wasn't sure why. Levi was gorgeous. He was tall, had dark curly hair, and brooding dark eyes. He was just the sort of man who was perfect for a movie poster. Plus, he had that sexy-rock-star thing already going for him. But he'd never shown an interest in acting. Not in the years they'd dated, anyway.

Things had obviously changed.

Gripping the wheel of his Tesla, Silas pulled to a stop in

front of his house situated on the mountainside. He'd had the modern house built to his specifications, and if he hadn't once lived there with Levi, he'd have been thrilled to be back. But now, despite the fantastic view of the Keating Hollow valley and the river that ran through town, Silas just found the place depressing.

He put the car in Park and ran inside. A moment later, he returned to the car with Cappy on his heels. After opening the back door, he waved for his rambunctious golden retriever to get in. "Want to go see Aunty Shannon?" he asked his dog.

Cappy wagged his tail so hard Silas feared the dog would strain a hip.

"Go on. Get in, or I'll leave your furry butt behind," he lied.

Cappy let out a high-pitched, excited whine and climbed clumsily into the car.

Silas let out a laugh and shook his head. "You goof." Then when Cappy lunged for the front seat and the takeout he'd left there, Silas shouted, "No, Cappy! That's not for you."

The golden retriever froze and gave Silas his best sad-puppy-dog-eyes look before curling up in the back seat as if he'd never tried to devour the risotto.

"Yeah. You're not fooling anyone, buddy." Silas climbed into the driver's seat, glanced back at his dog, who was now sitting up and slobbering all over the back window, and just laughed. It's what one signed up for when they decided to share their life with a golden retriever.

Ten minutes later, Silas pulled into Shannon's driveway next to her red Mustang. With the takeout in one hand and Cappy's leash in the other, he strode up to her front door and knocked.

No answer.

He knocked again and rang the doorbell.

Nothing.

Knowing that his sister often sat out beside the pool when working, he tried the doorknob, finding it unlocked. He let Cappy in and then followed, calling out, "Shannon? Dinner's here!"

He'd just placed the takeout bag on the counter when he heard a shriek come from the backyard. Silas hurried over to the sliding glass door and found Cappy jumping up on his sister as she hurriedly tried to cover her naked body with a long white dress.

Brian, her husband, was tugging on his jeans.

"Oh hell. Sorry!" Silas called and hurried back into the kitchen, feeling his cheeks burning with embarrassment.

"A phone call would have helped avoid this situation," his brother-in-law said as he strode through the back door, tugging on his T-shirt.

Silas gave Brian a flat stare. "I did call. At lunch. I left Shannon a message to let her know I'd bring dinner."

"Oh." Brian just shrugged and eyed the takeout bags. "What are we having?"

"There's crab risotto and Shannon's favorite, fried green tomatoes with remoulade." He walked over to their wine rack and pulled out a bottle of red. "I'm having this. What are you having?"

"That's fine," Brian said as he washed his hands in the sink.

"I hope you have more, because a glass or two isn't going to be enough after this day." Silas stared at the cork. A second later, his air magic forced it out of the bottle. The cork went flying and pegged Brian in the back of the head.

"Hey!" Brian rubbed at the spot where he'd been hit. "Was that necessary?"

"Yes," Silas said, pouring himself a generous glass. "I was too impatient to look for the corkscrew."

Shannon appeared, her cheeks tinged pink. Her long auburn hair was tied up in a messy bun that went perfectly with the flowy, white bohemian-style dress she was wearing. "Um, sorry about that. I guess time got away from us."

"I guess so." Silas took a deep swig of wine and leaned against the counter.

"How was it, seeing Levi again?" Shannon asked, placing a soft hand on his arm.

"Awful." Silas closed his eyes and recalled the hug he'd given Levi. "And amazing."

"Oh, Si," she said and wrapped an arm around his shoulders, pulling him in for a side hug. "Did you two talk?"

"A little. We're going to try to be friends."

Shannon let out a tiny snort of laughter.

Silas opened his eyes and glared at his sister. "This isn't funny. You know I have to make this work, one way or another. It's going to be torture acting this new script out with him."

"New script?" Shannon asked with her eyebrows raised.

He nodded and pulled the bound pages from his back pocket. "It's even more emotional and heart-wrenching than the last one."

"They just sprung this on you today?" she asked, flipping through the pages.

"Yes. At the table read." He downed another gulp of wine.

Shannon scanned the pages while Brian plated their meals and set the table. His brother-in-law led him to his chair and refilled his glass without Silas even asking.

"Shan," Brian said. "Your dinner is going to get cold."

She nodded and shuffled to her seat, never once taking her eyes off the page.

Brian and Silas shared a knowing glance. When Shannon was in work mode, getting her attention was impossible. Brian filled his own wine glass, held it up to Silas's, and said, "Good luck, brother. You're gonna need it."

"You can say that again."

After the toast, Brian dug into his meal, making appreciative noises while Silas barely even tasted the food that made it into his mouth. Instead, he studied Shannon as she took in the script. When he saw her wipe away a tear, he tossed the fork down and let out a groan. "Seriously? You're crying?"

"It's just... so good," she said with a sniff. "You don't see it?"

Silas pressed his fingers into his eye sockets, wishing he could have a do-over. "I don't know. I guess," he admitted. "It's just—"

"Painful?" she finished softly. "Too close to home?"

He nodded. "Yeah. That."

Shannon reached across the table and covered her brother's hand with hers. "I'm sorry, Silas. I wouldn't have recommended this to you if I'd known it would end up like this."

"Yes you would've. And if you hadn't, you'd have been a bad agent," he said, knowing in his gut that was true. Shannon was always on his side, and to her credit, she always knew when something was going to be a hit. "It's a damned good role, and I'd have been a fool to pass it up."

Sighing, Shannon put the script to the side, reached across the table with her other hand, and held on tightly to both of his. "You do know that your mental health and wellbeing is more important than any job, right? Just because there's a good opportunity on the table, that doesn't mean you need to take it."

Silas swallowed hard and nodded. But the truth was he hadn't been willing to turn down anything that had been a good move for his career. Not since he'd asked Shannon to take over as his manager from his mother all those years ago. His mother had been a celebrity hound, wanting him to take any role that would keep him in the public eye. Even things like reality shows, which he'd steadfastly refused and absolutely hated.

When Shannon stepped in, she'd made sure he had opportunities for solid acting roles. Interesting, quality roles that meant he was a respected actor, one of which had even landed him an Oscar. She was always looking out for his best interests, not her own. Completely opposite what his mother had done his entire childhood, always making sure he had one job lined up after another so that the checks kept rolling in whether he was interested in the roles or not.

Would Silas have passed up this opportunity if he'd known Levi was going to be his costar?

Hell no.

The answer was right there, screaming at him from his subconscious. But was that because he wanted to work with and be close to Levi? Or was it because he was so intent on building his career with the *right* projects that he wouldn't have been able to turn it down even if he wanted to?

He just didn't know.

And that was the entire reason Levi had broken up with him. Silas had always made time for the next project, the next job, the next big thing, but he'd never made sure he was there for Levi.

If a miracle happened and the time they spent together on

this movie actually brought Levi and Silas back together, would Silas be able to change? Would he prioritize his relationship over the demands of his career?

Could he?

He didn't have an answer, and that fact tore him up inside. That question was moot, though, because Levi hadn't shown any interest in rekindling things. Hell, they hadn't even spoken in more than two years. Two long, painful years.

"Do me a favor?" Shannon asked.

"What's that?" Silas met her compassionate gaze.

"Think about where you want to be in ten years. What does that look like? And more importantly, whatever you're doing, who's with you?"

"You," he said automatically.

Shannon rolled her eyes while Brian let out a groan.

"There's always going to be a danger of you walking in on us when we're about to have pool sex, isn't there?" Brian asked with a glint of amusement in his eyes.

"Pool sex?" Silas asked, grimacing. "I'm never getting in your pool again."

Brian laughed. "Mission accomplished."

"Hanging out with your sister all the time isn't going to do anything to improve *your* sex life," Shannon said with a smirk. "I suggest you reconsider your options." She winked at him and then dug into her risotto as if she hadn't eaten in days.

"Looks like pool sex works up an appetite," Silas said.

"Oh, no. There was no pool sex today. My brother-in-law cockblocked me," Brian said and went to open another bottle of wine.

"He's not going to let that go, is he?" Silas asked Shannon.

"Nope. Now, tell me everything. What did Levi say? How did he look? Why is he suddenly acting?"

Silas waited until his glass was full again and then sat back and sighed. "He's gorgeous. Talented. Angry. And apparently doing this because the opportunity fell into his lap and he couldn't say no."

"Angry?" Shannon asked, her eyes dancing with excitement. "At you?"

"Why do you look so pleased by that?" Silas barked at her. "Do you enjoy witnessing my torture?"

"Because, little brother," she said with a sly smile, "if he's angry, he's not over you. And I'm willing to bet my entire year's commissions that he's not doing this just because it's a good opportunity. He's doing it because you're here."

"That's not how he's acting," Silas said unhappily. "He looked like he wanted to punch me."

Shannon chuckled. "I bet he does. But that doesn't mean he doesn't *want* you. Trust me, Silas. This is your chance. If you want him back, show him you can give him what he needs."

"What if I can't?" Silas asked, his voice barely a whisper.

"All he needs is a partner who puts him first. Ask yourself, what's more important? Levi, or putting everything you have into an acting career that was never all that important to you in the first place?"

If that was the question, Silas would've been able to answer in a heartbeat. But what Shannon didn't realize was that acting was his entire identity. If he didn't have the career he'd carved out for himself, then what? Who would he be?

No one.

His mother's words echoed in his mind.

Silas Ansell, mark my words, you're going to be someone someday.

How many times had he heard her say that all he had to do was work hard and he'd have the world at his fingertips?

Could he give up everything for Levi?

He wanted to say yes. His heart screamed for him to do just that.

But deep down, he just didn't know if he could walk away from everything he'd built for anyone, not even himself.

CHAPTER 3

L evi paced his sister's backyard. The table reading that morning had been intense and unsettling. What had made him think he could act? It had become increasingly clear that all the emotion he'd shown while reading the script hadn't been an act at all. And while sometimes that had worked for the scenes, during others, it had been an epic fail.

Like when they'd read through the sweet parts of the romance. River and Ezra were taking a hike in the woods and got caught in a freak snowstorm and ended up spending the night in a hunting cabin. It was that scene when they first realized they had feelings for each other. The scene was supposed to be tender and romantic and then bittersweet when they had to go back to the real world. Instead, Levi had voiced it with the inability to hide his resentment.

Levi just hadn't believed that the characters would ever get past their hang-ups and issues. It didn't take a genius to understand that in some ways the script mirrored his relationship with Silas, and that's why he just couldn't seem to pretend that everything would work out in the end.

He'd given everything he had to his relationship with Silas. Even though they'd spent so much time away from each other, working on their respective careers, he'd always been there for Facetime chats and scheduled visits. He'd even turned down an interview with Rolling Stone because they tried to reschedule it when he was supposed to be with Silas.

Had it been a surprise to anyone that Silas had been the one who'd ended up canceling their weekend? No one but Levi. He'd been so naive. That's when Levi had started to understand that he'd never be as important to Silas as Silas was to him. And the resentment had started to creep in.

Shaking his head, Levi did his best to shut down his thoughts. He had work to do. Somehow, he had to start seeing Silas as Ezra and not the one who'd treated him as an afterthought.

Opening the envelope that had come just an hour before, he scanned the scene that they'd be working on the next day. It was a fight scene where River walks away from Ezra after a misunderstanding about a quote given to the press that causes a media shitstorm for River.

Levi let out a sigh of relief. Anger he could do. He had plenty of that to spare. It would be the makeup scene they did another day that would push Levi to his limits.

"Ohmigod, there you are!" Frankie, his foster niece, called as she hurried into the backyard, her face bright with adoration. The thirteen-year-old had come to live with his sister and Chad two years ago. "I can't believe you're home for three whole months. What do you want to do first? There's a harvest festival this weekend with a talent contest. You'd be a shoe-in for that. Also the farmers' market. There's a new booth that offers packaged gag spells, like candies that turn your voice high-pitched like helium, hot chocolate that gives people gas that makes them belch like a frog, and twirlers that spell out insults. That kind of thing. Which do you want to do first?"

"Um…" Levi didn't want to do either of those things. He'd never liked practical jokes, and there was the whole thing about consent when it came to edibles. "How about you do the talent contest and I'll cheer from the front row?"

She frowned. "I'm not good enough for a talent contest. Besides, I'd never feel comfortable up in front of a crowd. But you're a huge rock star. No one could beat you."

He stared at the eager young teenager. Her curly hair had been pulled back into a thick braid, and she was wearing an oversized T-shirt with skinny jeans. Everything about her was understated except for sequined red sneakers that sparkled when the setting sun shone on them. He could just tell there was a performer in her somewhere.

Levi took a seat on the porch swing and indicated for her to sit next to him. "Why do you think I should enter the talent contest?"

"Why not? You'll win for sure. All you'd need is your guitar and a microphone." She sighed wistfully. "What I wouldn't give to have spirit magic. Your ability to play almost anything is just… well, magical."

Levi chuckled. It was true. His spirit magic gave him an advantage when it came to learning instruments. He picked up the skills needed to play them quickly. Considering he'd spent the last three years touring, that little bit of help had certainly come in handy. Still, without practice, he'd never be as good as the greats. "You don't need magic to be a great musician. Most are not spirit witches," he said gently.

She frowned. "I know. I just get so frustrated. And all Chad says is that I'm doing great. But I still can't play 'Blackbird' without messing up."

"'Blackbird' is what you're using to assess your skills?" He gave her a rueful smile. "You know that song is deceptively hard. It's why Chad has you playing it. It'll help you lay down a foundation of skills."

She pressed her lips together in a tight line, clearly unhappy with the direction the conversation had taken. "It doesn't matter. I'm not entering that contest."

"That makes two of us then," he said easily.

"But—"

Levi held up a hand, stopping her. "Life isn't all about winning, Frankie," he said gently.

"I know but—"

"A talent show is for people who don't have other venues to get noticed. I've played all over the world. Have videos with millions of views. Why would I want to upstage someone who is just starting out or looking for recognition for their hard work? I don't want or need to win anything. I just want to hang out here, do this movie, and spend time with my family."

"Oh. You missed Hope and Chad, didn't you?"

"And you," he said, tugging lightly on her braid.

Her big eyes were glassy as she quickly glanced away. But when she turned back to him, she was all smiles and said, "Then Saturday it is. We'll go to the harvest festival and the farmers' market."

"You saw your opening and took it, didn't you?"

She shrugged.

"All right. But no gag spells. And I think you should sign up for the talent show," he challenged.

Her face paled as she shook her head.

"What if I get up there with you?" he asked with a raised eyebrow.

Her eyes narrowed as she pierced him with her stare. "But you said talent shows are for other people."

"They are. This would be for you. Show off that voice of yours. We'll both play the guitar. You sing."

She shook her head. "Not unless you sing with me."

"Backup only," he offered.

She was silent for a moment and then nodded once as she put her hand out. "Deal."

His lips twitched as he took her hand in his and shook on it. "Now get out of here. I have work to do."

Begrudgingly, she slipped back into the house, leaving Levi on his own to finally run his lines.

He was out there for an hour, working on delivery and memorizing his lines. Levi was determined to walk on set the next day fully prepared. He'd just delivered the line, "It's time for you to go," when he heard hooting and hollering from an upstairs window.

Glancing up, he found Frankie and one of her school friends videoing him. He let out a loud groan and then bellowed, "Frankie! Get down here. Bring your friend and that phone. Now!"

The back door slid open and Hope poked her head out. "Levi? What's wrong?"

He pointed to the two girls who'd just slammed Frankie's window closed. "It appears I can't even get away from the paparazzi in your house."

"What?" she asked, her face scrunched up in confusion.

"The girls were filming me while I ran my lines."

Hope pressed a hand over her eyes and muttered a curse. "I'm sorry. I'll handle it."

He shook his head and walked into the house, stopping at the bottom of the stairs just as Frankie and the blonde, curly-haired friend were trying to make a break for it. "Hand over your phones."

Frankie and the other girl looked at each other briefly. Then they shook their heads. "We already deleted the video."

"Let me see your phones," he said again. "I'm not asking."

Frankie let out a sigh and handed him her phone. The case was covered in skulls with one small kitten off in the corner.

"Unlock it, please."

"You know this is an invasion of my privacy, right?" she asked, sounding defiant even as she did what he asked.

"And filming me without my knowledge isn't?" he shot back and then checked to make sure she had deleted the video. "Did you send it to anyone before you deleted it?"

Her cheeks flushed pink.

"Frankie?" Hope asked, using her mom voice. "Who did you send it to?"

"Just a boy at school. He didn't believe me when I said that Levi is my uncle."

Levi wrapped his hand around the back of his neck and hung his head. That video would be viral by morning. He knew that Frankie hadn't meant to cause any trouble for him, but the fact was there was going to be a media frenzy when it was discovered. And the studio wasn't going to be very pleased either.

"I'm sorry, Levi," she said, her voice shaking. "I'll try to get him to delete it."

"Thanks," he said, walking away so that he wouldn't say anything he would regret.

He overheard his sister telling Frankie's friend it was time to go as he sequestered himself in the guest room. He sat on the bed and shot a message to his agent, warning him. His phone rang instantly.

"Yeah," Levi said into the phone.

"This can't happen again," Dawson said.

"I know. My sister is handling it," he said, wondering if that were true. While Levi was certain Hope would make it clear that invading his privacy was unacceptable, she couldn't exactly ensure that Frankie wouldn't make any other mistakes. With the last three years of touring and the fact that Levi was making a movie with his ex, the amount of interest in him was off the charts. If Frankie brought her friends around or talked about him at all, it was likely to end up in the papers.

His agent indicated he'd handle the producers of the movie but then said, "I think you need to get your own place."

"I know," Levi said. The truth was, he needed his space. As a spirit witch he could sense other people's energy, and he'd known that sooner or later he'd have to move out just for his own sanity. "There just aren't a lot of places to rent around here."

"Find something. It will help smooth things with the execs."

Levi ended the call, climbed onto the bed, and stared up at the ceiling. When he thought about moving out, the only place that came to mind was the house on the side of the mountain that he'd shared with Silas.

"*Dammit*," he muttered to himself and rolled over, groaning into the pillow.

Coming home had been a huge mistake.

CHAPTER 4

*S*ilas clicked on the video one more time and winced. It's wasn't as if he'd been scouring the internet for gossip about Levi. Silas was a firm believer in never googling himself. But when Shannon sent him the link, he hadn't been able to resist.

He almost wished he'd never watched it. As an actor, he knew and understood what it was like when he was trying to figure out how he wanted to play a character. One of his exercises was to do the lines a number of different ways until something felt right. Levi had watched him do that countless times. And it's what Levi was doing in the video.

Unfortunately, it was just a small clip of a line that clearly wasn't working. And now there were all kinds of comments complaining about Levi being cast in the movie. There was speculation about the producers casting him only because he was Silas's ex and they wanted to create buzz.

In a word, it was a nightmare.

He picked up his phone and sent a text.

Silas: *Are you okay?*

Levi: *I'll be fine.*

Silas: *Of course you will. That doesn't mean the negative press doesn't suck in the moment.*

Levi: *It's not the first time. I'm sure it won't be the last. It's the price of celebrity, right? Isn't that what you always used to say?*

Yes. He had said that. But he remembered what it was like for Levi when the pair of them had been hounded by the paparazzi when they first got together. He'd hated it. Levi didn't thrive on attention like some celebrities. He was into music for the art. And Silas had to assume he was doing the movie for the same reason. Having all this attention on him had to be wearing Levi down.

Silas: *I just wanted you to know I'm around if you need to talk or want to get lost in the woods for a few hours.*

The dots on the phone that indicated Levi was typing appeared. Then they disappeared. After a few minutes, they didn't appear again, and Silas tossed his phone to the side, frustrated. So much for being friends. He flopped down onto his couch and then immediately stood. If he stayed in his house for the rest of the day, he'd never get out of his head.

After packing a backpack with water and snacks for both him and Cappy, he grabbed his keys and called for his golden retriever. When Cappy saw the hiking harness, he let out an excited whine and spun around, barely able to contain himself. Silas grudgingly smiled down at his dog, knowing he'd made the right choice. At least one of them would be happy by the end of the day.

"Come on, Cappy. Let's go do something to work off this frustration so I don't eat my way through the cupboards."

The dog glanced back at the kitchen as if he was remorseful that eating everything in the cabinets wasn't an option.

Shaking his head, Silas led the way out of the house. His

dog reluctantly followed him, but when Silas opened the car door for him, he had a change of heart and flung himself into the back seat. Living with a golden retriever was never dull.

Twenty minutes later, Silas pulled into the parking lot of his favorite trailhead and then swore under his breath when he spotted the lone red Jeep and its owner climbing out of the driver's seat. Silas's eyes met Levi's, and when Levi scowled, it just pissed Silas off. He pulled in right next to Levi and hopped out, smiling at Levi as if this development was a pleasant surprise instead of a royal pain in his ass. "I guess the idea of a hike was too good to pass up."

"I'm not hiking today," Levi said as he placed his backpack into the back seat of his Jeep.

Silas raised an eyebrow. "You're not?"

"No. I, uh… I just went for a drive and found myself here. I guess it's just too busy at my sister's house. You know how I need silence every now and then."

"Sure," Silas said with a nod as he let Cappy out of the back seat.

The golden retriever ran straight for Levi, jumping up on Levi's chest and wagging his tail hard enough to throw a hip out.

"Hey, boy. I missed you," Levi said, his eyes crinkling at the corners as he gave Cappy a genuine smile.

The smile that Silas hadn't seen in over two years. Silas sucked in a sharp breath and busied himself with getting his own pack out of the Tesla. After he clicked the button to lock it, he turned around and found Levi holding Cappy's leash out to him.

"You two have a good hike. I'm gonna take off," Levi said.

Silas glanced down at the old familiar hiking boots on

Levi's feet. "Interesting footwear," he said, shaking his head. "So much for being friends, huh?"

"Silas..." Levi started.

But when he didn't say anything else, Silas just tugged on Cappy's leash. "Come on, boy. It's just you and me today."

Silas could feel Levi's eyes on him as he and Cappy started out on the trail. After they stepped into the trees, he heard the door to the Jeep slam and the vehicle roared to life. He paused, waiting until the sound of the Jeep's engine faded in the distance.

His anger started to vanish, and a deep sadness crept in. The truth was, he missed Levi. More than he'd realized. It was easier to put the memories away when he was busy working or fretting about his next role. Now that Silas had to see him every day, putting the past behind him seemed impossible.

Cappy ran ahead of Silas and about a half mile in, he jerked free of his leash and took a sharp left onto a smaller trail. The one that led to the watering hole.

Son of a... Silas's heart ached even more when he realized where Cappy was leading him. Of course he was. Cappy loved the water, and he and Levi had taken him there every chance they'd had back when Cappy had been a puppy.

Reluctantly, Silas made his way down the path. When he stepped into the clearing, he spotted Cappy swimming in the clear blue water, splashing and playing with wild abandon.

Silas sat down on a rock near a waterfall and waited for his dog to tire himself out. It wasn't long before the memories crashed over him, and he was taken back to the first time he and Levi had visited the spot. They'd still been teenagers, but even then Silas knew something special and rare was happening.

There was a chill in the air, but Silas barely felt it. He was too focused on the young man who was following right behind him. Levi was a welcome reprieve from the world Silas lived in. For as long as he could remember, he'd been surrounded by people who were hyper-focused on getting their big break. When they weren't all backstabbing each other for the same roles, the majority of the conversation seemed to always be about beauty secrets, diets, or workout plans. If he had to hear one more time about how amazing someone's plastic surgeon was, Silas knew he'd be tempted to poke out his own eardrums.

Levi was so different. He intrigued Silas. Fascinated him. He was real. An old soul who cared about the people around him. He was the first person Silas had met in a long time who'd wanted to get to know Silas the person, not Silas the actor.

"That's it," Levi said from behind him, pointing through the trees.

They walked into the clearing, and Silas felt a sense of calm wash over him.

"This would be a great swimming hole if it were the middle of summer," Levi said, leading Silas over to a flat rock near the edge of the lagoon.

Silas let his gaze wander over Levi, imagining him wet and dripping after he dove into the water.

Levi's lips turned up into a slow smile, no doubt guessing that Silas's thoughts were less than wholesome. "Care to share what's going on in that mind of yours?"

Chuckling softly, Silas grinned. "I'm sure you can figure it out."

"Hmm, I suppose I can." Levi pressed his shoulder against Silas's and then reached for his hand. "It's a little cold for that though."

"It's okay," Silas said, staring at their entwined fingers. "I like these quiet moments with you."

"You do?" Levi asked, sounding curious.

"Yeah. All of the noise of my life slips away and..." Silas paused,

31

trying to put his feelings into words. "When I'm with you, everything feels right. Like I've finally found home."

Levi was silent for so long Silas started to wonder if he'd said something wrong. "Levi?"

"Yeah." He wiped away one tear that had slid down his cheek.

"I'm sorry. I didn't mean to—"

"No." Levi cut him off. "Don't apologize. What you said, it means everything to me. You have to know that, right?"

Silas swallowed hard. Before he could answer, Levi spoke again.

"I've never had anyone besides Hope love me. It wasn't until I came to Keating Hollow that I even started to feel like maybe I wasn't going to end up in jail or on the streets for the rest of my life. My sister Hope saved my life. But you... You make it worth living. You're my home, too, Silas. You have been for a while."

Bringing his hand up to cup Levi's cheek, Silas stared him in the eyes and for the first time ever, he said, "I'm in love with you."

Tears welled in Levi's eyes as his throat worked. Finally, in a gruff voice, he said, "It's an honor to love you, Si. It's just scary, you know?"

Silas nodded because he understood. His childhood hadn't been as traumatic as Levi's, but he had his own issues to work through. "I've never had anyone want me just for me and not care about the celebrity. Promise me that won't change."

"You don't have to worry about that," Levi said, his voice full of conviction. "But I need something from you, too."

"Anything."

"Promise me that when this is over, you won't just walk away from me. That our friendship will survive."

"Walk away from you?" Silas asked incredulously. "What makes you think I'd do that?"

Levi averted his gaze as his cheeks reddened. "It's what people always do."

"Hope hasn't," Silas pointed out.

"True, but she knows what it's like to be thrown away," Levi said. *"We understand each other."*

Pain shot through Silas's heart for what Levi had been through and how it had affected him. He placed both hands on Levi's cheeks, holding him tenderly as he said, "No matter what, I will always be here for you. Understand?"

Cold water sprayed over Silas, yanking him out of his memories, and he jumped up, shrieking, "Cappy! What the hell?"

The dog was standing right next to him, shaking the water out of his coat and spinning around in excitement. He finally came to a stop at Silas's feet, staring up at him in adoration.

"You goof." He held out a treat to his dog. After Cappy wolfed it down, Silas put his leash back on him and jerked his head toward the trail. He needed to shut down memory lane immediately. "Let's go, buddy. Let's get in that hike before we both get soft."

Cappy trotted ahead of him, leading him away from the lagoon, the memories, and the guilt that plagued Silas for breaking his promise to Levi. Sure, Levi had broken up with him, but Silas hadn't made any effort to remain friends. He'd done exactly what Levi had been afraid he'd do. He'd thrown away their friendship because he'd been hurt and let his pride get in the way. And now it looked like he was too late to repair it.

Frustrated with himself, he gritted his teeth and stared blindly ahead, hoping that the hike worked off some of his bad mood. He needed to get his head on straight before he walked on set the next day, otherwise, he knew he'd never be convincing for the cameras. Not unless they did a fight scene or the one when Ezra and River parted ways.

33

He followed Cappy onto the main trail and started to head up the mountain. But he'd only gotten about ten feet when Cappy started snarling and tugging the leash. The dog shot forward, lunging for a bobcat. Silas, who was still holding the leash, was pulled right off his feet and landed in the dirt face-first.

With the wind knocked out of him, Silas groaned and rolled over, rubbing his aching shoulder. He glanced around, making sure the bobcat wasn't ready to pounce on him. The trail was clear, no cat in sight. There also wasn't a golden retriever.

"Cappy!" Silas called as he pushed himself to his feet, only to stumble and fall backward onto the trail as pain shot through his ankle, nearly making him black out. He grasped at his joint as if that would stop the pain.

It didn't.

He breathed through the pain for a long moment and then looked down at his rapidly swelling ankle and cursed.

CHAPTER 5

*L*evi felt like an idiot. Obviously Silas realized he'd been at the trail to go hiking. But when Levi saw his car pull into the small parking area, he'd panicked. It had been a rough couple of days with the video of him going viral.

The studio was pissed. They'd said it would've been one thing if it showcased Levi's acting chops, but instead, it showed him delivering a line that was not just bad but *comically* bad. The kind of clip people would be laughing about for years to come if Levi stayed in the public eye. It meant he didn't just need to be good in the movie, he needed to be brilliant, or else the offers would never roll in again.

On the one hand, he hadn't ever dreamed of being an actor. On the other, he kind of liked the break from touring. It was fun to pretend to be someone else for a while.

Mostly he just wanted to stay away from the internet and pretend none of it was happening. That was why when Silas had mentioned a hike, he'd decided a solitary walk in the woods was exactly what the healer ordered. Too bad Levi hadn't arrived just ten minutes earlier. He'd have been on the trail and none the wiser when Silas showed up.

Not wanting to go into town or home to deal with Frankie, who was riddled with guilt and spending most of her time trying to do everything and anything she could for Levi to make up for her mistake, Levi parked at an undesignated spot along the river. He could search the trail app on his phone for somewhere else to hike, but he knew most of the other trails near town were busier and more likely to have other hikers around. He wasn't in the mood to talk to anyone. The trail he and Silas had both chosen was one that was more out of the way and didn't lead to any of the known attractions, such as Keating Hollow Ridge or the Winding River Trail. It was just trees and that small lagoon that had somehow been spared from being marked on the tourists maps.

The sun was high in the sky, but the light breeze gave him a chill, causing him to grab his jacket from the backseat. On a whim, he pulled out his guitar, too. He'd decided to start taking it with him to the set so that he had something to settle his mind when he needed to get into character. There was something about strumming the strings that seemed to pull him out of his head, making it easier to act.

He made his way over to a fallen log near the river and sat down. The sound of the water flowing over an outcropping of rocks was just as soothing as music, and he sat there flexing his cold fingers, just listening to nature. He felt his shoulders begin to relax, and the tension he'd been carrying around with him started to ease.

This what he'd needed. Some space away from everything to just take in the beauty of the forest. There didn't seem to be any other place for him now that made him feel settled like he did in that moment. Silas's house had been that for him at one time, but now... He imagined he'd only feel pain and regret if he went there.

The act of holding the guitar made his fingers twitch with the desire to play. Settling on an old favorite, he picked out the chords and sang softly to himself.

"Dark days, sleepless nights, struggling to find my way. And then there you were, your name bright in Hollywood lights. You saw me when no one else did. I loved you for you without caring about what you do. Winter nights turned into sunny days. City lights turned to magical fog-soaked bays. If only we'd held on, you'd still be by my side. Instead, I'm here, living in the darkness of my mind."

Levi trailed off, letting the words of the song he'd been working on fade away. His heart ached, and he started to wonder if he'd ever finish it. The words had been rattling around in his mind for months, but it wasn't until he'd come back to Keating Hollow that he'd actually started to put them to music. Every time he tried to write them down, he stared at the blank page and eventually gave up, not sure if he was ready to canonize his pain.

But he knew he would eventually. That's the way it was with him when he heard a song in his head. If he didn't get it out, it'd never leave.

With his head bent, he lost himself in the chords and hummed along, trying to find the rest of the song. When his fingers were almost numb with cold, he finally put the guitar aside and stood, intending to walk down to the water. But before he could move, he felt a sharp stab of fear in his gut.

Fear that wasn't his.

The energy was familiar. He'd know it anywhere.

Silas.

Grabbing his guitar, Levi ran back to his Jeep and jumped

37

in. Without even thinking about it, he sped back to the trail where he'd left Levi just an hour ago. The Tesla was right where Silas had left it, still locked.

"Dammit." Levi grabbed his pack that had water and a small first aid kit and then took off up the trail, following Silas's thread of energy. The fear had been overshadowed by frustration and pain, but it was still there under the surface.

Levi quickened his pace, worried about what he'd find when he reached Silas. His lungs were burning and his legs ached, but he pressed on, desperate to find him. The only thing that kept his panic at bay was the fact that Silas's energy was so readable. As long as Levi could find him, he was certain everything would be okay.

A dog barked in the distance.

"Cappy!" Levi called as he rounded a bend in the trail.

The yellow dog came sprinting toward him. When Cappy reached Levi, he immediately spun around and headed back up the trail, clearly leading Levi to Silas.

"What happened, Cappy?" Levi asked.

The dog didn't look back as he ran around another curve in the trail.

When Levi finally caught up with Cappy, the golden retriever was standing at the edge of the path, barking incessantly.

Silas was nowhere to be found. The only evidence anyone had been there recently was a disturbance in the dirt that led over the edge into the brush.

Levi scanned the area, noting where the brush had been cleared away by a fall, and then he quickly scrambled down the side of the hill, calling, "Silas! I'm here."

"Levi?" Silas's surprised voice called back to him.

Levi finally spotted the red of Silas's jacket and knelt down to find him covered in mud and scowling. "What happened?"

"What does it look like happened? I fell down the side of the hill."

"Okay," Levi said carefully, scanning him for injuries. It didn't take long to spot the softball-sized ankle. Levi winced. "That looks painful."

"Why do you think I'm still sitting here?" Silas spit out.

"I figured you were just being dramatic," Levi said dryly as he pulled the first aid kit out of his backpack.

"Yes, because I've been known to wallow in mud."

Levi reached for Silas's foot, gently turning it to inspect the damage.

Silas yelped and swatted his hands away. "Please don't. Just help me to my feet so we can get out of here."

"You're not going anywhere with your ankle like that," Levi said, holding an ACE bandage. "Let me—"

"I said I'd be fine," Silas said stubbornly. "All I need is a hand."

Levi sat back on his heels and stared at Silas. His ex knew he had healing abilities. If Silas would just let him work his magic, he'd be on his feet in no time. Not completely healed, but he'd at least be able to hobble out of the woods without too much pain. "Why won't you let me help you?"

"I just..." Silas waved a hand and then blew out a long breath. "I don't know. Honestly, my ankle hurts like hell."

"I bet it does. If you're willing, I can do something about that. Then we'll get you out of here so you can warm up. Maybe get a shower?"

Silas's eyes met Levi's at the mention of a shower. Their gazes lingered for a long moment before Silas tore his eyes away and nodded. "Do it."

Levi had to suck in a deep breath to clear his mind. He did not need to be thinking about Silas in the shower. "I'm going to need to touch your ankle, but I promise to be gentle."

Silas gritted his teeth and nodded. "Do what you have to."

"Try to relax." Levi carefully slid a little further down the hill so that he could easily reach Silas's ankle. Then he placed both hands on the swollen flesh. His fingers tingled with red-hot heat. It was the trauma from the injury. All Levi had to do was suck the heat out, and the ankle would quickly be on the mend.

Before Levi's music career took off, he'd trained with a healer in Eureka. It turned out that Levi's spirit magic gave him some unusual abilities. One of them was healing people. He'd thought about working as a healer professionally, but there was an emotional toll for using his healing energy, and he knew that if he made a career out of it he'd burn out faster than a match in a wind tunnel. These days, he only used his magic to heal someone when it was an emergency. Otherwise, the cost to his mental health was too great.

With the lightest touch possible, Levi focused on Silas's ankle and imagined the blood rushing to the torn ligaments, rapidly speeding up the healing, and then he willed the fiery heat of the trauma to seek his fingertips. Instantly, his fingers turned to fire as the trauma poured into him.

Levi's stomach turned sour, and a headache formed above his left eye. But by the time he lifted his fingers off Silas's ankle, the swelling had gone down considerably and the joint was no longer hot.

"How are you feeling?" Levi asked him.

"Like an idiot," Silas said, all his irritation gone.

"Sure," Levi agreed. "But I meant, how's your ankle?"

"It's throbbing less. I suppose I won't know until I try to

walk. Help me up?"

Levi stood and held out his hand.

Silas grabbed on with both hands and pulled himself up onto the uninjured foot. He glanced up the hill and groaned. "This is going to suck balls, isn't it?"

Levi smiled at him. "And not in the good way."

Chuckling, Silas shook his head and then tentatively tested his weight on his ankle. He grimaced and let out a hiss, but he was able to put at least a little pressure on it.

"Come on," Levi said. "Better to crawl up the hill and then I'll help you down the trail."

"Wonderful," Silas grunted. "So glad I'm going to keep my dignity."

"Just be glad it's only me and not the paps." Levi jerked his head. "Go on. The sooner you get up that hill, the sooner we can get you home and into a shower." Silas raised one questioning eyebrow, making Levi chuckle. "Get up the hill before Cappy loses his mind."

The dog was whining, desperate for Silas to reappear.

"I'm coming, Cap," Silas said and then crawled back up the hill, grumbling the entire way.

Once they were back on the trail, Levi wrapped his arm around Silas's waist and said, "Lean on me. I'll get you back to the car."

Silas just nodded, and together they slowly made their way down the trail. By the time they got to Levi's Jeep, Silas was sweating and swearing under his breath. "Dammit, that hurts."

Levi opened the passenger door to his Jeep and said, "Get in. I'll take you home."

"I can drive," Silas said, shuffling toward his Tesla.

"Your right ankle is turning purple, Si. Just get in the Jeep. I'm sure Shannon and Brian can come get your car, or I'll get

Hope to help me and we'll get it for you. Driving isn't an option."

Before Silas could say anything, Cappy jumped into the Jeep and curled up in the back seat, obviously exhausted from the ordeal.

Silas gritted his teeth and gave Levi a short nod. "Fine."

"Fine?" Levi echoed, rolling his eyes. "How about a thank you? If I hadn't listened to my spirit magic, you'd still be at the bottom of that hill." As soon as the words were out of his mouth, Levi wanted to shove them back in. He hadn't meant to sound so self-centered. He didn't need Silas's undying devotion because he'd come to help him. He just wished Silas wasn't so caustic about the situation.

"Are you saying that if you'd known I was going to be so ungrateful that you'd have just left me there?" Silas challenged.

Levi shook his head. "Just get in the Jeep, Silas. You know damned well I'd never leave you there, even if you are being a major pain in my ass."

Silas's lips curved into a tiny amused smile. "I always did love getting under your skin."

"Keep it up and I won't stop for dinner on the way home."

Home. The sound of the word on his lips nearly ripped his heart out. Levi missed living with Silas. There was no denying that. They'd been really good at sharing space. The trouble started once they were both living out of hotels for their respective jobs.

"I could go for some dinner," Silas said softly and then hauled himself up into the Jeep.

Levi carefully closed the door, sucked in a long breath to steady himself, and hurried to climb into the driver's seat. "Burgers?" he asked.

Silas's eyes gleamed as he nodded.

The sun was starting to set as Levi called in the order to the Keating Hollow Brewery. Squinting at the fading light, Levi put the Jeep in gear and headed for town.

They were both silent for the first few miles, and then Silas cleared his throat.

Levi glanced over at him, briefly meeting his gaze before focusing on the road again. "What is it, Si?"

"Thank you," Silas said, his voice gruff.

"I'm just glad I was there to help."

Silas let out a small bark of incredulous laughter. "That, right there. That's why I fell for you."

Startled, Levi jerked his head in Silas's direction. "What?"

"What do you mean, what? I meant exactly what I said. You're so selfless, always there for the people you love. You live to take care of the people around you. There's no BS or insincerity. You're just you and honest to a fault. Do you know how rare that is, Levi?"

"Rare? That might be overstating things," Levi said with a nervous chuckle. He really didn't know how to respond to Silas's declaration. Why was he talking about that now, anyway?

"Trust me. It's rare." He paused for a moment and then added, "I'm probably going to regret standing you up for the rest of my life." He gave Levi a sad, forced smile. "But we can't change the past, can we?"

Levi's chest was tight as he nodded his agreement. "I've yet to master time travel."

Silas sighed. "Same. If you figure it out, will you let me in on your secret?"

That made Levi chuckle as he said, "You'll be the first to know."

CHAPTER 6

$\mathcal{T}$he moment Levi pulled into Silas's driveway, Cappy started to whine.

"Relax, boy," Silas said, patting his head. "Give us just a second, okay?"

Levi jumped out and opened the back door for Cappy, and Silas watched as his dog ran around in a circle then jumped up on Levi before taking off to make his rounds around the property.

"Your dog has enough energy to power the entire town," Levi said as he walked over to help Silas out of the Jeep.

"I've got it," Silas said, waving him off. It was one thing to accept his help while trying to get off the trail, but he could manage the few feet to the porch, where, thank the gods, there was a railing to hold onto.

Levi held his hands up in a surrender motion. "Was just trying to help."

The irritation in Levi's tone should have made Silas feel guilty for being difficult, but he just couldn't muster the will. It had been a long-ass day. He was tired, embarrassed, and just wanted a shower and a fresh change of clothes. After he hopped over to the front deck, he used the railing to pull himself up without putting too much pressure on his ankle. It still hurt, but at least he was sort of mobile.

Levi held back at his Jeep, watching with a frown on his face.

Once Silas was in the house, Levi followed him, bringing the food and his backpack and setting it all on his coffee table. He went straight to the kitchen and started making an ice pack.

"I can do that," Silas said, hobbling into the kitchen.

"I've got it." Levi handed him the pack and then went back for a glass of water and grabbed the anti-inflammatories from their spot in the cabinet to the left of the refrigerator.

Silas watched him, his heart aching at the sight of his ex moving around his space with comfortable ease. It felt *right* having him there. Even though he knew he should shut his emotions down, he just couldn't. More than anything, he wanted Levi to stay. To have dinner with him. Watch something on Netflix. Talk about anything and everything.

"Here. Take these." Levi handed him two pills and a glass of water.

Silas did as he said and let Levi position the ice pack on his ankle that was propped up on a kitchen chair. "Thank you. For everything."

"No need to thank me," Levi said as he hurried to the back door to let Cappy in. "I'll just feed him first, then I'll ask Hope if she can help me get your Tesla."

"You don't have to do that." Silas watched him, noting that his shoulders had tensed again and the ease he'd shown just a few moments ago had vanished. Now he just looked like he was ready to bolt. "I'll get Shannon and Brian to get it."

"Yeah. Okay." Levi dropped a scoop of food into Cappy's bowl. As he put the food away, he said, "You should call the healers' clinic. If they can fit you in, I'll give you a ride."

"Do you think it's broken?" Silas asked him. It was something Levi would have known after using his healing magic.

"No. Sprained for sure. Maybe a torn ligament. But Gerry might be able to help you heal faster."

Silas nodded and glanced at the clock. It was already past clinic hours. "I'll go in the morning."

"Do you—" they both said at the same time and then started laughing.

"You go first," Levi said, his face lit with a small smile.

"I was just going to ask if you wanted to eat in the living room. Maybe watch a movie?" He didn't add the last bit... *like old times*, but it was there just hanging in the air between them.

Levi's smiled dropped, and he cleared his throat before he said, "Thanks, but I better get home and prepare for tomorrow."

"You're not staying to eat?" Silas asked, a little stunned. He'd thought when Levi got them dinner he'd at least stay for a little while.

Glancing at his watch, Levi grimaced. "I'm sorry. I just..."

"It's fine. I understand." Silas waved a hand, hoping he looked unconcerned.

There was an awkward silence between them. Finally Levi awkwardly grabbed his burger from the bag, nodded once, and then walked to the door. "Good night, Silas."

"Good night, Levi," he said, deflated and feeling the sharp stab of rejection all over again.

"STOP! STOP! STOP!" Marcus, the director, called, clearly frustrated as he waved his arms in the air.

Silas stepped away from Levi and sucked in a long breath. The day was not going well. Both of them had been acting as if the day before hadn't happened. In fact, ever since he'd gotten to work, Levi had barely looked at him unless forced to do so during a scene. That had pissed Silas off. And more than anything, he just wanted the day to end.

Marcus walked over to Silas and placed his hands on his hips. "Now remember, Silas, your character doesn't have any family," he said. "Your mom surrendered you to the state when you were only four, and your dad gave up his rights shortly after. You grew up in the system and were on your own at eighteen. Imagine what that does to a person."

Silas couldn't help it when his gaze landed on Levi. He looked frustrated, but Silas was certain he was the only one who noticed. It was the tension in his hands, Levi's tell when he was trying not to show his emotions. He was sitting in a chair, his eyes closed and his head propped against the wall behind him. The details were different, but Marcus's description of Silas's character wasn't unlike what Levi had gone through as a kid right up until Hope and Chad had taken him in.

Levi glanced up, meeting his eyes and then glaring at him, no doubt knowing exactly what Silas was thinking. If there was one thing Levi didn't want from him, it was pity. Though Silas hadn't ever pitied him; he admired him. Levi had gone through more than most people by the time he'd turned seventeen and had ended up a caring, thoughtful man with a gigantic heart of gold.

A familiar dull ache materialized in Silas's chest, and he

rubbed at his breastbone as if that would make it go away. He knew from experience it wouldn't.

"Yeah, got it," Silas said, turning his attention back to Marcus.

"Good, so you understand why Ezra has trust issues, right? Why he doesn't truly believe that River will stick around?"

"Because of the demands of his job," Silas said automatically.

Marcus gave him an exasperated look. "No. It's because he doesn't believe he's worthy of love. No one has ever loved him enough to stay. With that in mind, do the scene again."

Silas let that sink in for a long moment and had to force himself not to look at Levi again. If he did, he didn't know what he'd do or say. In that moment, he needed to get himself into the mindset of Ezra and become the character.

"Rolling!" Marcus called.

Silas stood at the window that was supposed to look over the Puget Sound, staring at the sunrise.

"I'm not going to sign it," Levi said from somewhere behind him. "I already told my mom no."

Silas turned, letting his gaze settle on the rock star who'd just turned down millions of dollars because Ezra had declined to go out on the road with him due to an important art installation opportunity he'd been offered from the city of Seattle. "You can't do that," he said, his voice cracking. "Not for me."

Levi moved until he was standing behind him, wrapping his arms around Silas. "I can, and I did. Don't you get it, Ezra? I don't want to go. Not now. The tour can wait until it's the right time for both of us."

Silas turned and met those gorgeous brown eyes, shaking his head. "I won't let you turn this down. It's too important.

You're on the verge of a major career-defining moment. If I'm the one who..." He frowned. "You can't say no. You just... can't."

Confusion flickered in Levi's gaze as he took a step back. "If you're the one who... what?"

Silas threw up his hands in exasperation. "You'll resent me if I'm the reason you don't go. That's what. If you don't want to go, then don't. But do it for you. Not me. All right?"

"Cut!" Marcus called. "That's better. Everyone take fifteen while we work on changing this lighting."

Silas was shaking when he walked away from Levi. How many times had Levi told him not to make career decisions based on what Levi was doing? That they'd work out their schedules and meet when they could. Had Levi been pushing him away the entire time? Never letting Silas take Levi into account when he decided to take a role or not? It had happened at least a dozen times.

It had been their thing. To never hold each other back. And they hadn't.

Not once.

Silas took the roles he was interested in, and Levi went off and turned into a rock star. They were ships passing in the night. It was why Silas hadn't thought too hard about standing him up when there was something important going on with his career.

Had Levi been testing him?

If he had, Silas had failed miserably.

"Hey, are you okay?" asked August, a PA he'd worked with before when he'd filmed in Befana Bay. August normally had an easy smile and a kind word for everyone. The frown on his face was almost alien to Silas.

"Yeah." Silas ran a hand through his hair and sucked in a deep breath. "Was just caught up in the moment, you know?"

"Sure." August held out a water bottle to him and flashed his trademark smile. "It can't be easy filming with an ex."

Silas let out a sardonic laugh. "That's an understatement."

"If it's any consolation, I don't think it's any easier on him." August gestured to Levi, who was sitting against the wall, his eyes closed and his shoulders hunched up with obvious tension.

"It's really not," Silas said. And then, deciding he needed to be around people other than just his sister and brother-in-law, he added, "Thanks, August. It's nice to have a friendly face around here. Maybe we can get coffee after filming ends today if it's not too late?"

"Sounds good. I'll need to finish some things up when we wrap tonight, but I shouldn't be too long. Should I meet you at Incantation Café or…"

"Just knock on my trailer door. If it's too late for coffee, we'll go get some beers."

"You're on." August nodded to one of the wardrobe people and said, "I'm being summoned. Good luck on the scene."

"Thanks." Once August was gone, Silas glanced over at Levi and let out a sigh. He really did look to be struggling. Grabbing the cane Healer Whipple had given him that morning, he made his way over and slid down the wall, sitting next to Levi. "Acting can really take it out of you. I imagine it's sometimes like that with certain songs."

Levi opened his eyes and stared at him, not saying anything. Finally, he nodded. "Yeah. It can be. The personal ones."

"It's why we do what we do though, right? Love and

connection is a universal experience. Giving people something to relate to is the ultimate gift."

"If you say so." Levi glanced at Silas's foot. "How's your ankle today?"

"Still sore, but Healer Whipple worked her magic and I can walk on it without too much trouble. She gave me this cane to use for the next few days, but she said I can put my full weight on it if it's not too painful. So I can film without limping, but until it's fully healed, I'll be using this when the cameras aren't rolling."

Levi nodded. "That's good. I'm glad you were able to see Gerry this morning."

"Me, too." Silas wasn't sure what else to say. Had it been a mistake to join Levi? His ex wasn't being hostile, but he didn't exactly look comfortable either, judging by his pinched expression.

Levi sucked in a breath, and his next words came out in a rush. "I think I need to apologize."

Startled, Silas twisted to really look at him. "For what?"

Levi turned so that their faces were only inches apart.

Silas wanted desperately to reach out and cup his face, but he kept his hands to himself.

"I should have stayed last night. Had dinner at least." Levi's face flushed pink. He was flustered, but he didn't avert his gaze like he usually did when he was uncomfortable. "That's what friends do, right? They are there for their friends when they need them. They don't just run out of the house because..." He waved a hand as if to clear the air of his thought. "Anyway, I should have stayed."

"It's all right," Silas said automatically, though Levi's abrupt departure had left him feeling rejected and a little bit sorry for himself.

"It's not," Levi said firmly. He chewed on his bottom lip before continuing. "That scene back there... I think it hit far too close to home for both of us."

"Yeah," Silas said with a nod. "Probably."

"Anyway, I think maybe everything that went down between us wasn't all your fault, and I've been acting like it was." He held Silas's gaze, his eyes searching.

Silas wasn't sure what to say to that. He knew that Levi had left him because he was tired of being stood up. And Silas definitely had not made Levi a priority. Not when he was so worried about his career. But maybe Levi had made that easier for him by always insisting that he never factor Levi into his decision-making. "It takes two to make a relationship work. And two to ruin it, I guess. You don't need to apologize. I get it."

The tension in Levi's shoulders slowly seemed to ease as he forced his hands apart. After swallowing hard, he gave Silas a tentative smile. "Can we maybe start over?"

Silas's pulse kicked into overdrive. Was Levi suggesting that they try again? That maybe their relationship wasn't dead and buried? It was on the tip of his tongue to say yes. Definitely. He'd try again. But then Levi spoke, taking all the air out of the room.

"As friends, I mean. I know we already said we'd work on that, but I really want to give it a try. Maybe spend some time together outside of work? I don't want us to just be cordial while working together. It would be a lot easier to get through this movie if I didn't feel so... I don't know, awkward and unsure of what to say to you. I think maybe if we tried to put the past behind us, it would be easier."

For him maybe. That sounded like torture to Silas, but he found himself nodding anyway. The truth was he missed Levi.

Not just his boyfriend, but the person. Levi was smart and funny and sensitive. He'd been a calming force in Silas's crazy life. And even though Levi had his own level of fame and pressures to deal with, Silas was willing to bet he'd still be that same calming force for him. If it was friendship or nothing, Silas would take friendship. "Yeah. Friends. *Real* friends. I'd like that."

Levi's lips curved up into a relieved smile. His eyes were bright, and his entire body seemed to relax the way it used to when they were together. It made that ache in Silas's chest fade just a little bit more. "Good. That's good," Levi said and then put his hand out. "To being friends. For real this time."

Silas took his hand just like he had a few days before, felt that familiar rush of connection, and held on, unwilling to let go. Levi didn't seem to be in a hurry either as they got lost in each other as if they were under some sort of spell. If someone had asked Silas in that moment, he'd have insisted they were. The rest of the world fell away, and the only thing that mattered was the man sitting next to him.

"All right everyone. We're ready for you," one of the PAs called.

The spell shattered.

Levi quickly pulled his hand back and got to his feet. "Come on, Ezra. There's another scene to do."

"Yeah, River needs to pour his guts out. Good luck with that," Silas said.

Levi let out a humorous laugh. "I'm gonna need it."

CHAPTER 7

"You can't be serious," Levi said, staring at the all too familiar house on the side of the mountain.

Wanda, his realtor, gave him a sheepish look. "I know it's not ideal, but it's literally the only rental available in town. And we're lucky this one is free. Amelia and Grayson just moved into their new place overlooking the river yesterday. If they'd moved last week, no doubt someone from the movie production would have already gotten it."

Most of the people working on the movie were either staying in short term rentals, at the Keating Hollow Inn, or they were commuting from Eureka, the nearest town that was over thirty miles away. Housing was always difficult in Keating Hollow. It's why most people who moved there ended up buying land and building. It's what Silas had done.

Levi sat back in Wanda's SUV and covered his face with his hands as he let out a groan. "I can't be living right next door to my ex while also working with him for the next three months."

Silas's house, the one Levi had lived in with him right up until they'd broken up two years ago, was right behind the small three bedroom that would be absolutely perfect for his stay in Keating Hollow, if only it wasn't a hundred feet from his ex. It was one thing to try to be friends with Silas. It was entirely another to be walking distance from his bedroom at all times.

"I know it isn't ideal," Wanda said, her tone sympathetic. "But it's not like you'd be living *with* Silas. Are you sure you don't want to at least take a look at it?"

There really wasn't any point. Levi had been in the house a number of times. Amelia and Grayson were friends of his. Still, he figured since they'd driven all the way out there it was only polite to let Wanda show him the house. "Yeah. I guess."

"Great. I think you might change your mind once you see the upgrades that have been made recently." She pushed her door open and climbed out.

The upgrades didn't make a difference. Levi already knew he was going to have to say yes to the rental. The noise on social media about the viral video hadn't died down, and the studio was threatening to fire Levi if anything like that happened again. Especially now that there were predictions that the movie was going to tank, all based on a fifteen-second low-quality video of him trying out different ways to deliver lines.

The last few days had been humiliating to say the least.

Frankie was devastated and kept begging him not to move out, but that wasn't an option.

"Levi?" Wanda called from the porch. "Are you coming in?"

With a sigh, Levi climbed out of the SUV and followed Wanda up the steps and into the small house. The view from the front window was just as spectacular as he remembered. The house sat on the side of the mountain, overlooking the town of Keating Hollow and the river that ran through it. To the north there was another mountain range, and if he was lucky, by Christmas the peaks would be snow-capped.

"It's gorgeous, right?" Wanda said.

He nodded.

"This is what I wanted you to see." She waved for him to follow her into the kitchen area, but she didn't stop there. She walked out onto the back porch and swept her arm out with a flourish as if presenting him with the hot tub that was nestled into a pretty gazebo.

Levi took it in, and then his gaze locked on the yellow creature that was barreling toward them, his ears back and his tongue lolling to the side.

"Cappy!" Levi said, his heart swelling with love for the golden retriever. The dog ran full speed straight for Levi and jumped up, his paws hitting Levi's pecs as he knocked him down onto the ground and then slathered him with kisses.

"Oh my gosh! Levi, are you okay?" Wanda called out as she rushed to his side.

"I'm fine," Levi said with a laugh, scratching the dog's ears. "How are you doing, boy? Did you miss me? It's only been a few days, you silly creature." When Levi glanced up at Wanda, she was staring down at him with an amused smile.

"Well, it looks like at least one of the neighbors would be happy to have you here," Wanda said.

"Cappy's not the only one," Silas said, seemingly coming out of nowhere. "Cappy, off!" he ordered the dog and then held out a hand to Levi to help him up.

Levi stared at Silas's outstretched hand and contemplated ignoring it. The last two times they'd touched, the connection had been undeniable. Reliving that experience was going to get harder and harder as time went on. But Levi had meant it when he'd told Silas he wanted to be friends.

Brushing off his offer to help would be a step in the wrong direction.

"Thanks," Levi said, clasping his hand around Silas's. That zap of electricity sparked between them, and Levi almost snatched his hand back just to maintain his own sanity. But Silas held on tight as he pulled Levi to his feet, only letting go after Levi cleared his throat and tugged.

"Sorry," Silas said, looking a little sheepish.

Levi ignored his apology as he shoved his hands in his pockets. "Your dog could use some obedience classes."

Silas raised one eyebrow. "Yeah?" Then he turned to Cappy, the fluffiest dog on the planet and said, "Sit."

Cappy obeyed instantly.

"Lie down."

The dog stretched out in the small patch of grass.

"Roll over." Silas mimicked the movement with his hands, and Cappy rolled over, putting his legs in the air and playing dead. When Silas snapped his fingers, Cappy jumped back up and sat patiently at Silas's feet.

"That's impressive," Levi said. "You two have definitely done a lot of work since..." He cleared his throat, unwilling to voice anything about their breakup. "Since before I went on the road."

"We've had a lot of time together the past six months," Silas said softly. "Befana Bay has a dog trainer who works magic. Literally."

"So you did finally take Cappy to training classes." Levi gave Silas a flat stare. It was one of the things Levi had wanted Silas to do, and he'd always said he was too busy. Silas had been too busy for everything. Including Levi.

"Yeah. You were right about that. Cappy likes the discipline, and the only time he gets out of line is when he's too excited to contain himself. I think it's obvious he likes having you around."

It was on the tip of Levi's tongue to ask if Silas liked having him around too, but he clamped his lips together and swallowed the question. That was not something that needed to be out there.

They were going to be *friends. Just friends.*

"Well, Cappy," Levi said, reaching down to scratch the pup's ears, "I'm just as happy to have you around, too, buddy. I'm looking forward to giving you lots of hugs and belly rubs."

The dog leaned into Levi's leg, giving him what Levi always assumed was the dog's version of a hug. Levi grinned, and for the first time in a long time, he felt at home.

"Are you renting this place?" Silas asked, his tone sounding hopeful.

Or was that just wishful thinking on Levi's part? Surely Silas hadn't been pining away for Levi for two years. If he had, he'd have reached out, right? But since the pair had broken up, Silas hadn't called Levi. Not even once. He hadn't even returned Levi's call after that one night when Levi had broken down and left a message with Silas's PA.

Living right next to Silas was a terrible idea. Despite his predicament with the studio and his living situation, Levi opened his mouth to say no, but Wanda spoke first. "He's still thinking about it."

Silas raised one eyebrow, piercing Levi with his stare. "What's there to think about?"

The statement was a challenge. Silas would know that the only reason Levi would turn down the rental was because it was right next to Silas's house. "I'm just weighing my options," Levi said.

"Well, don't think too long, Levi," Wanda said. "Since it's the only rental available, I expect it to go very fast. In fact, I'm pretty sure the new owner has already gotten a few inquiries, but if I tell her you're interested, you'll be a shoe-in. You know, being Keating Hollow royalty and all."

Levi let out a derisive snort. "Royalty? That's a little over the top, don't you think?"

Wanda just shrugged. "Local boy makes it big on the music scene and is the darling of the media? No, not over the top. The people of Keating Hollow are proud of you. Charlie isn't going to rent out her house to someone from LA who's here to work on the movie when she knows you're looking."

Darling of the media. Not anymore. Not after that video went viral. But Levi didn't correct her.

"The only rental on the market?" Silas asked, eyeing Levi with suspicion. "What are you waiting for?"

Called out and put on the spot, Levi knew that if he didn't take the house, Silas would know exactly why. And he couldn't give his ex that kind of power. Not when he had to work with him on a romantic film for the next three months. If he was going to make it through this movie, he had to make sure that Silas never found out that, despite everything, Levi still wanted him. So what if he had to torture himself knowing his ex was right next door every night? It couldn't be worse than acting out a love scene, could it?

Levi stifled a groan and then put on what he hoped was a nonchalant expression when he turned to Wanda and said, "I'll take it."

CHAPTER 8

"*A*ction!" the director called.

Silas steeled himself for the scene and did his best to ignore the cameras trained on him before slipping into the movie set dressing room. Levi was right on queue when he stepped out of the adjoining bathroom wearing only a towel. Silas let his gaze sweep briefly over his ex, taking in the new ripples of muscles defining his abs, and he had to suck in a breath to keep from gasping.

Damn, he looks good.

How many times had Silas fantasized about such a scene? And here he was, supposed to be acting it out. All those nights when Silas had been on location for a film and Levi had been out on tour seducing thousands of fans with his smoky vocals, Silas had imagined jumping on a private plane and surprising Levi after a show. Just hiding out in his dressing room and showing him how much he'd missed him.

"You're here," Levi said, his posture a little stiff as he said his line.

"I couldn't stay away," Silas said, forcing himself to move

toward Levi as he clenched his hand into a fist so he wouldn't be tempted to wipe the beads of water off Levi's golden skin. For the sake of his own sanity, he had to avert his gaze.

Levi cleared his throat.

"Cut!" the director yelled. "What is going on here? You two have about as much chemistry as a couple of rocks. This is supposed to be the scene when you finally admit your feelings for each other. How are you going to do the bedroom scene when you both look about as excited as a man headed for his annual prostate exam?"

"Sorry," Levi mumbled. "I think I'm just a little nervous. First time acting an intimate scene and all."

"What about you, Silas? What's your excuse? You're the pro. I want you nervous and excited. Not nervous and tortured as though you'd rather be anywhere but here."

Son of a... That wasn't at all what he was feeling. If anything, he was too worked up. The effort to keep himself in check was probably why he was giving off constipation vibes. "Sorry, Marcus. Just working out the kinks. Give me a minute and I'll be ready."

Marcus, the director, rolled his eyes. "Fine. Everyone take fifteen. But you both better be ready when we come back. Time is money, people. Time is money."

Silas wasn't too concerned about the budget. He'd worked with Marcus before, and the man had a penchant for shooting scenes over and over and over again to make sure the shot was just right. One could say he was obsessive about it.

Still, Silas knew he was off his game. It just figured that he'd wanted to film the payoff scene so early in the process. The one where the two heroes finally declared their love and ended up together. His character was supposed to be excited and nervous and ready to lay everything on the line for Levi... or rather River, the name of Levi's character.

Silas hurried out of the barn where they were filming at the Pelsh Winery and strode over to his trailer. He climbed in and flung himself onto the couch, knowing he needed to find a way to relax and get into character. That wasn't going to happen if he was looking around for Levi the entire time. The moment he thought of Levi, he remembered his stiff posture in the scene and cursed under his breath.

While Silas did need to find a way to get into character, if Levi couldn't relax and slip into his character too, the scene was going to be a huge waste of time. He glanced over at Levi's trailer. Wouldn't it be better if they worked on the scene together? Got comfortable with each other again?

That seemed like an impossible ask.

From the moment Levi had walked back into Silas's life, he'd felt off-kilter. Relaxing seemed damned near impossible. Especially since the only thing he wanted to do was grab Levi, crush their lips together, and force him to remember what they'd been like when they were together.

Though Silas knew better than anyone that the physical aspect of their relationship had never been the most important ingredient in what made them work. Kissing the hell out of Levi would probably only ratchet up the tension.

He had to do something. Anything to try to salvage the day. There was no time like the present. After guzzling down a glass of water, he gathered his courage and made the trek over to Levi's trailer. After knocking, he shoved his hands in his pockets and waited.

The door popped open and Levi stuck his head out. When his eyes landed on Silas, he frowned, looking confused. "Is it time to go back already?"

"No. I just thought we might want to try to work this out together before we start filming again."

Levi raised both eyebrows. "And how are we going to do that?"

Silas swallowed an exasperated sigh. "Can I come in?"

For a moment, Silas thought Levi was going to slam the door in his face, but eventually he stepped back and waved Silas in.

Once Silas was in and the door was closed, he glanced around and spotted Levi's guitar on the couch. "Do you play a lot on set?"

"I don't know if I'd say it's a lot," Levi said with a shrug. "Mostly when I'm trying to work through something."

Silas nodded as if he understood, but he didn't play any instruments, so he didn't really.

"So?" Levi asked. "What's the plan? Do you want to run lines or something?"

"No. I don't think that's our problem. I thought maybe we just need to get comfortable with each other again."

Levi sank down into one of the chairs and eyed Silas. "And how are we supposed to do that?"

Silas gave him a self-deprecating smile and then let out a chuckle. "Short of making out, I'm really not sure."

"That's what you're here for then?" Levi asked, his expression suddenly stormy. "You think if we just hook up then everything will be fine?"

"No," Silas shot back, suddenly heated. "That's not at all what I came here for, but if I thought shoving my tongue down your throat would ease the tension between us, then yes, I'd try it. It certainly couldn't hurt considering our chemistry in front of the camera appears to be nonexistent."

"You're saying that's my fault?" Levi's eyes were narrowed, and his voice was low and full of irritation.

"That isn't what I said." Silas gritted his teeth. "This was a mistake. I'm just going to go. Obviously, me being here isn't helping."

"Maybe you should." Levi got up and opened the door.

Silas hesitated for just a moment, wondering what in the hell had just happened. Everything had been fine between them the day before. Hadn't it? He'd run into Levi while he was with Wanda looking at the rental house. Levi hadn't acted like he was irritated then. What had changed? The challenging day on the set? "I'm sorry," Silas said. "I didn't mean to make it worse."

"You didn't." Levi blew out a breath and ran a hand through his hair, making it stick up all over the place. The stylists would be all over him the moment they got back on set. "I think I just need a minute with the guitar and then I'll be fine."

"Sure." Silas gave him a quick nod. "I'll see you back out there."

As soon as Silas stepped foot into the parking lot, Levi yanked the door closed with a loud thud, making Silas jump. He knew Levi wasn't having some sort of tantrum. It was normal to use some force to close the door, otherwise it wouldn't latch properly.

Just before Silas disappeared back into his own trailer, he heard the soft strumming of a guitar. He paused, listening to the song he'd heard Levi play many times before.

It was *their* song. The one Levi had written about them before everything had fallen apart.

His heart started to ache, making him rub absently at his chest. It didn't help. As long as he and Levi were apart, Silas knew that wound would never heal.

Shaking his head, trying to clear all his destructive thoughts, Silas climbed back into his trailer. Letting himself think about what he'd lost with Levi was the absolute worst thing he could do when he had to go back out there in less than five minutes and slip back into character to film a scene about getting everything he'd ever wanted.

CHAPTER 9

*W*hat *the hell is wrong with me?* Levi thought, so frustrated he was ready to walk right off the set. He couldn't get his acting together. Literally. And he was taking it out on Silas. Why hadn't he taken Silas up on his offer to work on the scene?

He knew why. The thought of kissing Silas and then acting out the love scene had sent his anxiety through the roof. How was he going to get through that scene without showing all his cards? Everyone knew he wasn't that good of an actor. Great musician? Yes. Actor? That was still up for debate. If he let his guard down, Silas would see right through him. He'd know that Levi hadn't ever stopped loving him.

Then what would Levi do? He'd spent the past two years working hard to be okay with his single status. Opening himself up to all those old feelings was going to ruin him.

Levi grabbed his phone and tapped out a text to his agent. *Get me out of this contract.*

The return text came almost immediately. *Are you serious this time?*

No. Just freaking out.

Do you need me to come to Keating Hollow?

Levi stared at the last text, feeling like a major drama queen. There was no way he was going to ask his agent to babysit him because he'd been too stupid to realize that doing this movie would mean he'd have to act intimate with Silas.

You knew. The words materialized in his mind, seemingly of their own free will. Apparently, even lying to himself was out of the question. Had he actually taken the role just to be near Silas? To touch him again?

No. He'd taken it to show Silas what he'd been missing.

Levi let out a groan, realizing that was the honest to goddess truth. He had signed on to prove to Silas that he was doing just fine. Only he wasn't. He was falling apart only days after they'd started.

No, he texted back. *Just needed to vent, I guess. Ignore me.* He put the phone down and rubbed his face with his palms.

Now what?

The only thing to do was to go back out there and pretend to be in love with his ex.

Pretend. Right.

A knock sounded on his trailer door. "Two minutes!"

Levi sucked down a few gulps of water, gritted his teeth, and made his way back to the set. The wardrobe assistant handed him the towel he was supposed to be wearing and gestured for him to use the makeshift dressing room to get back into character. It didn't take long for him to strip down to his boxer briefs and wrap the towel around himself.

After walking back onto set, he was doused in water to make it look as if he'd just stepped out of the shower. Before he knew it, the director was yelling, "Action!"

Levi heard the sound of a door opening and then walked

out of the fake bathroom into the room that was supposed to be his dressing room. He imagined what it would have felt like to see Silas appear after one of his shows while he'd been on the road. A slow smile claimed his lips, and his heart skipped a beat as he said, "You're here."

Silas's gaze raked over Levi, and he licked his lips before replying, "I couldn't stay away."

Levi watched Silas move toward him. He knew River was supposed to meet Ezra halfway, but Levi was rooted to his spot, watching wordlessly as Silas pinned him with his stare and moved as if he were stalking his prey.

When Silas's hand pressed against Levi's chest, the script called for Levi to put his forehead against Silas's as the two of them breathed each other in. Instead, Levi stumbled back, his entire body vibrating with tension. It was a physical response he couldn't seem to control. Instead of the tender moment the script called for, Levi buried his fingers in Silas's hair, both desperate to push him away and aching to kiss him. They stood locked there, just gazing at each other, neither of them able to continue the scene.

The director sighed heavily. "Cut!"

Levi immediately dropped his hand and took another step back.

Silas glared at him.

A multitude of unspoken words hung between them.

It felt to Levi like if he opened his mouth, everything he'd wanted to say over the past two years would just come spilling out in a jumbled mess. He pressed his lips together, forcing himself to remain silent.

Silas had other ideas. "Do you hate me *that* much? You can't even try to pretend to be happy to see me? I know you have it in you. Even the look on your face when you saw Cappy would have been better than... whatever that was." He waved his hand around, indicating the energy Levi had been giving off.

Levi raised both eyebrows. "You're one to talk. There was nothing tender about the way you were looking at me, Silas. I've seen less aggression on a lion's face."

"Enough!" Marcus ordered as he scowled at both of them. "You two. In my trailer. Now!"

Levi turned on his heel and followed the director, feeling Silas right behind him. He wanted to turn around and tell Silas to back off, but the less talking he did in that moment the better. He knew fighting with Silas in front of Marcus was just about the worst thing he could do.

Marcus yanked his trailer door open and stomped in. Levi followed and glanced around at the makeshift office. "Sit!" Marcus ordered.

Levi glanced at the small couch that was against the wall and did as he was told. When Silas sat right next to him, he did his best to pretend that Silas didn't even exist. Otherwise, he knew they'd only start fighting again. Either that or Levi was going to stick his tongue down Silas's throat, just to try to wipe away the tension that was pulsing between them.

"This isn't working," Marcus said, crossing his arms over his chest.

"I know, I'm—" Levi started.

"Stop. Just stop." Marcus paced the small space and then stopped to stare at them both. "I get that there are issues between you two. I'm aware you used to be in a relationship and honestly, sometimes that makes what happens on camera magic. We have some really stellar scenes already in the can due to this tension between you two. But what we saw today? That's not the kind of tension we need for that scene. I know you both know that. Since neither of you seem to be able to get

RETURN OF THE WITCH

out of your heads and get into the acting space that I need, here's what we're going to do."

Nerves rolled in Levi's gut as Marcus sat across from them and clasped his hands together.

Eyeing them with intensity, Marcus continued. "I'm going to send you two home early today and film some other scenes that don't include you. For the next two and a half days, you two will spend every moment together. And when I say every moment, I mean it. Stay in the same house, cook together, work on a song or the script. Something that makes you work together instead of ignoring each other. Whatever is going to make you comfortable around each other again. Then Monday morning, we're doing this scene again and you're going to make me believe that you're ten thousand percent in love and ready to risk it all for each other. Got it?"

Levi sat back, stunned. Could the director really order them to spend the next sixty hours together, doing things they would have done while dating?

"That's asking a lot," Silas said carefully.

"The studio is also paying you a lot to act like you love each other. If you can't do it your way, you'll do it mine. Got it?" Marcus asked.

"Yeah." Silas closed his eyes and took a deep breath as if willing himself to calm down.

Levi wasn't sure what he felt. There was a lot happening at the moment. He was humiliated that he hadn't been able to do his job. But he was also terrified of being alone with Silas for that long. How was he going to keep pretending that he no longer had feelings for him? A tingle of excitement replaced the nerves in his gut when he realized that he now had an excuse to spend two and a half whole days with Silas.

Dammit, Levi was a hot mess.

"Levi?" Marcus prompted.

"Yeah?" He looked up, almost surprised that Marcus was still there.

"You understand what I'm telling you? Go spend the weekend working out your issues and be back here Monday ready to work."

"Absolutely," Levi said and couldn't stop his gaze from landing on Silas.

His ex was staring openly at him as if trying to figure out what Levi was thinking.

Levi gave him a tiny smile and stood, turning to the director. "Anything else?"

"Nope," Marcus said. "Just make sure you don't waste this time. If we have this conversation again, it's going to involve studio execs and possible replacements."

Silas swallowed audibly and then said, "We'll be ready on Monday."

Levi just nodded, realizing that this was a make-or-break moment. The humiliation of being fired from the project was something he definitely didn't want to deal with, but he knew he'd survive it. Acting wasn't his passion. But it was Silas's, and he knew that his ex was probably panicking. Silas was a dedicated actor who took his craft very seriously. To have a director threaten to fire him from a coveted project would be devastating to him. It was that moment when Levi decided that no matter what, he would put everything he had into this movie. Not for himself, but for Silas.

CHAPTER 10

Silas followed Levi out of the trailer, stunned to his very core. Had that just really happened? Never in his professional life had he not been able to pull out a performance when he'd needed to. The very idea of being told he could be replaced mortified him. Above all else, Silas was a professional.

"Your house then?" Levi said, standing in front of him with his hands in his front pockets, shoulders hunched.

"My house?" Silas asked stupidly. For some reason, he'd imagined they'd stay at the rental. Being together in his house again for three nights while not really being *together* would be pure torture. Wouldn't it?

"Yeah. I don't really have any furniture yet. It's being delivered next week."

"Oh. Sure. My house." Silas was so thrown by the situation he was having trouble processing it all. "Right. Okay."

"Hey, Si," August, the production assistant, called as he walked by. "We still on for beers after we shut down today?"

Silas could feel Levi's eyes boring a hole into his head. "Um, not tonight. Sorry. Something just came up. Can we have a rain check?"

August looked slightly disappointed, but he nodded. "Sure, man. We'll try again next week."

"Definitely." Silas had really enjoyed having someone to talk to after work the last few days instead of spending every night at his house, alone with his memories. He'd even started taking Cappy to Shannon's house in the morning so that he wouldn't be home too long by himself.

"You're dating the PA?" Levi accused, his voice lowered to a hushed whisper.

Silas blinked and then turned to his ex. The anger on Levi's face pushed Silas's buttons and before he could stop himself, he shot back, "Why, is that a problem for you, Levi? I've been single for over two years now. What am I supposed to do, pine for you forever?"

"That's not—" Levi stopped talking abruptly then shook his head and turned around, stalking toward his trailer.

"Not what?" Silas asked angrily as he followed him. "Come on, Levi. Just say whatever you want to say. It's not like you haven't hurt me before. What's one more time, right?"

"I hurt you?" Levi asked incredulously. "That's rich, considering I was the one sitting at home alone, waiting for you when you were off at some party and networking for some show you never even got cast in."

Hushed whispers from behind them caught Silas's attention, and he swore under his breath. "Let's not do this here."

"I'm not the one who wouldn't let it go," Levi said and stalked off into his trailer. A moment later, he emerged with his guitar case and moved swiftly toward the parking lot.

Silas's shoulders hunched forward as he followed Levi,

wondering why he hadn't denied the dating accusation immediately. August was only a friend. And he was straight. Letting Levi think for even a minute that there might be something going on between them was just petty and not fair to August.

Levi stowed his guitar, jumped into his Jeep, and slammed the door. He had backed out and was leaving the parking lot before Silas had even retrieved his keys.

He sent Levi a quick text to let him know he was going to pick up Cappy and some food and would meet him at his house in about an hour.

Levi didn't text back.

SILAS HAD SPOTTED Levi's Jeep parked at the house he'd rented and assumed he was waiting there until Silas got home. When he opened his front door, Cappy nearly knocked him out of the way to get into the house. The golden retriever made a beeline for the kitchen, his tail going nine hundred miles an hour as he jumped up all over Levi.

"You're here," Silas said, his tone surprised.

"Where else would I be?" Levi looked up from his spot at the counter where he was busy placing cookie dough on a baking sheet.

"Your Jeep is next door and, well, you left your key here after things ended." That dull ache materialized in Silas's chest again, but he ignored it. Rubbing the area had never helped. There was no need to advertise his pain.

Levi raised one eyebrow. "I'm the one who hid the spare key, remember?"

Ah, the hide-a-key. "Right."

Frowning, Levi stopped working and stared at Silas. "Should I have waited until you got back?"

"No," Silas said immediately and shook his head. "I was just surprised, I guess." He gave Levi a tiny smile. "It's been a long time since I came home to anyone but Cappy."

Levi's expression turned guarded as he went back to scooping out cookie dough. "I'm sorry I ruined your date."

"What date?" Silas asked as their conversation about August came roaring back. He let out a groan. "August and I weren't going on a date."

"That's not what it looked like. Or sounded like," Levi said quietly, all of the fight having gone out of his tone.

"I know him from when we were filming in Befana Bay. He's just a friend. And he's straight."

"Oh." Levi's cheeks tinged pink, making Silas chuckle. Narrowing his eyes, Levi leveled his gaze at Silas. "It's not funny."

"It kind of is. Jealousy looks good on you."

Levi snorted. "I'm not jealous."

They both knew his declaration was a lie, so Silas just let it go as he placed the takeout he'd gotten on the counter. "Are you hungry?"

"I guess." Finished with scooping out the cookie dough, Levi placed the baking sheet into the already preheated oven.

"Snickerdoodles?" Silas asked as he grabbed plates from the cabinet.

"What else would I make?" Levi asked, his lips quirking up into that secret smile that he'd always saved for Silas.

The dull ache in his chest that had been nagging Silas vanished immediately. "I can't wait."

Levi leaned over and peered into the food bag. "What did you get?"

"Lasagna."

The look on Levi's face turned to pure adoration. "You, my good sir, are an angel."

Silas had debated on whether he should pick up the dish, knowing it was Levi's favorite. He hadn't wanted to appear like he was trying too hard. But in the end, he knew it was what Levi would pick if he was ordering for himself, so he went for it. The fact that Levi had been making Silas's favorite cookies told him he'd made the right decision. Maybe this weekend together was exactly what they needed to find some stable footing again.

"Wine?" Silas asked, already moving to grab a bottle.

"Sure."

They worked together setting the table, and Silas found himself more content than he'd been in over two years. The familiarity they had and the fact that Levi was so comfortable in his home was everything. Silas found himself wishing that Levi would stay forever. This was the life he'd wanted. The one he'd had but messed up beyond repair.

They sat down to eat, and immediately Cappy placed his large nose on the table.

"Cappy, lay down." Silas pointed to the floor, and the dog very slowly lowered himself, giving Silas his big brown puppy dog eyes.

Levi snorted. "He's laying it on thick, isn't he?"

"Anything to con you out of a bite." Silas winked.

The air between them thickened as their gazes locked. The easy rapport they'd found slipped away, and all Silas could think about was how he didn't ever want Levi to leave. He wanted to live in this bubble forever.

Levi averted his gaze, staring down at his meal.

"Levi?" Silas said tentatively.

"Yeah?" Levi jerked his head up, trying and failing to conceal the sadness in his expressive eyes.

All Silas wanted to do was wrap Levi in his arms and somehow magically erase the past. But even in a world filled with magic, time travel still wasn't possible. Instead, he just needed to own his mistake and try to move forward. "Do you think you'll ever forgive me?"

Levi's eyes widened as his mouth dropped open slightly. He quickly closed it as he recovered and gave Silas a side-eye glance.

"Never mind," Silas said quickly, shaking his head. "Don't answer that. It's way too soon into the weekend for that kind of heavy conversation."

To Silas's surprise, Levi chuckled, his eyes lighting with humor.

The weight bearing down on Silas's chest disappeared, and suddenly he started to believe that maybe, *just maybe*, they actually would be able to become friends again.

"You never could filter your thoughts around me," Levi said, digging his fork into his lasagna. "It's one of the things I always loved about you. I always knew what you were thinking."

Loved. Past tense. Another arrow to the heart. Silas gave him a forced smile and then dug into his pasta. If he was going to spend a platonic weekend with the love of his life, then he seriously deserved some comfort food. Calories be damned.

They ate in stilted silence, not even talking when the timer went off and Levi got up to remove the cookies from the oven.

The scent of cinnamon and sugar filled the air, making Silas's mouth water. He wanted to abandon his pasta and dive headfirst into the cookies he knew Levi had made just for him. Instead, he focused on the lasagna and tried to ignore the fact that despite their silence, he hadn't been this content in ages.

When Levi finally put his fork down, he leaned back, pressing his hands to his stomach. "Looks like I'm going to need to spend some extra time on the treadmill this weekend."

Silas raised a questioning eyebrow. "Treadmill? I thought you didn't like working out on machines."

"I don't." Levi grabbed their empty dishes and carried them to the sink. "But when you're traveling from hotel to hotel and different cities for months at a time, it's hard to map out a decent running path. It's just easier to head to the gym."

"Unfortunately, my treadmill is out of commission," Silas said with a frown. "I think there's a short in the wiring."

Levi shrugged. "No problem. I can head to the gym in town."

"What if we took a drive out to the coast in the morning and went running on the beach?" Silas offered.

"Together?" Levi asked, blinking at him.

Silas chuckled. "Well, yeah. We're supposed to spend the entire weekend together, right? It'd give us something to do at least."

"Uh, right," Levi said with a slow nod. "Yeah, okay. That sounds like a plan."

"Great. What time do you want to go? Six?"

Levi groaned. "You and your early mornings. Does it have to be six?"

"The earlier we go, the better chance we have to avoid paparazzi." Silas poured the last of the wine into their empty glasses. "But if you don't mind our pictures being splashed all over the tabloids, we can go any time you want. Ten?"

Levi clutched his wine glass and with a grimace, he said, "Six it is."

Silas let out a tiny snort, knowing that would be his answer. Then he nodded to the cookies cooling on a wire rack. "Are those fair game, or were you planning to eat them all yourself?"

"Just eat your cookies, Silas. You know I made them for you." Levi rolled his eyes and went back to loading the dishwasher.

Silas picked up a handful of cookies, but before he shoved one into his mouth he said, "Hey, Levi?"

"Yeah?"

"Thank you."

CHAPTER 11

*L*evi stepped out of the shower and wrapped a towel around his waist. After he'd finished the dishes, he'd quickly headed for the shower, needing some time to collect himself. He still couldn't get Silas's question out of his mind.

Will you ever forgive me?

Levi once thought he had. Or at least had tried to. But it was glaringly obvious he hadn't. Not really. He was still hurt that Silas had chosen his career over him.

Maybe if he understood why, then Levi could get past it. But he didn't. He didn't think he ever would. He just couldn't imagine choosing work over his person. Especially when Silas already had a thriving career. He didn't need to jump through hoops in order to finally get his chance. Silas was an Oscar winning actor for the goddess's sake.

Levi pressed his hands flat on the vanity countertop and hung his head. One way or another, he had to suck it up and figure out a way to bury the hatchet, because no matter what else he felt, he really did want him and Silas to be on good terms. Movie or no movie, being resentful for the rest of his life sounded miserable. That was no way to live. Besides, even if he and Silas weren't meant to be together, Levi had learned something over the past week. He still cared about Silas and wanted the other man in his life, even if that only meant friendship.

Friends had never been easy to come by. Not for Levi. His spirit magic made it so that he was sensitive to other's emotions. Most of them were too overwhelming for him. But Silas's never had been. Not even now when Levi could sense that his ex was full of regret and frustration. But Silas also exuded warmth and caring and a purity of soul that just soothed Levi. Being around him was... comfortable. He didn't want to give that up.

A knock sounded on the door. "Levi?"

He jerked his head up and stared at the door. "Yeah? Is everything okay?"

"Sure. It's just that your phone has been blowing up for the last ten minutes. I figured you might want to check it out."

Frowning, Levi reached over and opened the door. Silas stood there with Levi's phone in his hand as he slowly lowered his gaze, taking in Levi's half-naked body.

Despite himself, Levi couldn't help the tiny smile that curved his lips. It had been a long time since he'd felt desired. Sure, there were always fans who screamed for him or who'd be happy to join him in his dressing room, but Levi wasn't into hookups or one-night stands. He'd always craved the company of someone he really cared about.

And that person had always been Silas.

The last time Levi had been with anyone, it had been the man who was standing in front of him, staring openly at his abs. Sure, he'd been on a couple of dates, but neither of those had turned into anything. It was hard to give anyone else a chance when Levi was still in love with his ex.

Levi cleared his throat.

Silas jerked his gaze back to Levi's face, a pink flush tinting his cheeks. "Sorry." He quickly handed the phone over and spun on his heel, retreating from the bathroom door.

Chuckling, Levi watched him go and then walked across the hall to the guest bedroom where he'd stashed the bag he'd brought for the weekend. Before he pulled fresh clothes out of his bag, he checked the phone. There were no less than ten messages from Frankie, one from Hope, and two from his agent, Dawson.

He groaned, tossed the phone down and then got dressed. Once he was no longer just in a towel, he went through the messages. The ones from Frankie were about finalizing plans for the next day.

Saturday. The day he'd promised to take her to the farmers' market and participate in the talent show.

"Dammit," he muttered, having forgotten all about his promise to Frankie after he'd been ordered to spend the weekend with Silas. There was no way he'd skip out on their day together if he could help it.

Before he texted Frankie back, he called his agent.

"There you are. I've been waiting to hear from you all day," Dawson said as soon as he answered.

"It's been a little… crazy today," Levi said, sitting on the edge of the bed.

"So I heard. Are you all right?"

The fact that Dawson actually cared how Levi was doing instead of just worrying about how much money Levi could generate was the reason he'd hired the man. "Yeah. I'm fine. A little freaked out but otherwise okay. I assume you heard that

Marcus ordered me and Silas to spend the weekend together?"

"I heard." Dawson's tone was full of irritation. "You know he can't force you to do that, right? If you need me to get you out of this, I will."

But did he want to get out of spending the weekend with Silas? The answer was an unequivocal no. "It's fine. Really. I think it will help us."

There was silence on the other end of the line.

"Dawson?" Levi asked.

"I'm here."

"Why are you being so quiet then?"

There was a rustle of sound on Dawson's end before he said, "You haven't looked at the headlines yet, have you?"

Levi swallowed a groan. "No. You know I try to stay away from the internet these days."

"Then I think you should know there's a pap shot of you letting yourself into Silas's house. The rumors are already swirling that you're back together."

"Seriously?" Levi pressed his hand to his temple, trying to ward off a headache.

"Yes. Do you want to issue a statement or just ignore it? If you two lay low, this will probably blow over fairly quickly."

Even though Dawson couldn't see him, Levi shook his head, resigned to the fact that the media wasn't going to leave them alone no matter what he said. "No. I'm not interested in explaining anything to anyone. Just ignore it. But you should know I'm planning on spending the day with Frankie and Silas tomorrow. I'm sure that won't help the rumors. But really, who cares? I bet the studio will be eating it up. The more publicity we get, the more hype for the movie, right?"

"That's one way of looking at it. How does Silas feel about it?"

"I guess I'm about to find out." Levi thanked his agent for the information and then ended the call.

After scanning the messages from Frankie and Hope, he pocketed his phone and went out into the living room to find Silas staring at his own phone, a pained expression on his face.

"How bad is it?" Levi asked him.

Silas turned the phone around, revealing the headline.

Love on and off the screen. Shacking up after only a week of filming.

"It could be worse," Levi said, taking a seat on the couch next to him.

"Sure. It could always be worse." Silas's frown deepened. "If I wasn't obsessive about keeping the blinds closed, they could've already had a shot of you in your towel."

Levi snorted and waved at his slim frame. "No one wants a picture of me in just a towel."

Silas raised one skeptical eyebrow. "Seriously? You really don't have any idea how sexy you are, do you?"

Levi glanced away, certain this wasn't a conversation they should be having. "Anyway..." He let out a chuckle and said, "Let's just be glad all they have is a picture of me walking in the front door."

"Now that they have a story, there will be a lot more than just that one picture unless we go into hiding." Silas eyed Levi, his expression curious.

Suddenly, the situation just seemed ludicrous to Levi. Both of them lived their lives in the public eye. Neither were strangers to the paparazzi pictures. But it had always puzzled him that the media always seemed to be more interested in their dating lives than anything else. Why was everyone so interested in whether they were dating or not? The truth was, Levi just didn't care if they wanted to run stories about him and Silas. It was better than constantly recycling the humiliating video of him trying out different versions of his lines.

Levi turned to Silas. "What do you think about really giving them something to talk about tomorrow?"

"You're not suggesting we open the blinds and let them have towel shots, are you?" Silas teased.

"No," Levi said with a laugh. "After everything that happened today, I completely forgot I promised to spend the day with Frankie tomorrow. Since we're supposed to spend the entire weekend together, I thought that if you didn't mind tagging along, I wouldn't have to cancel on her."

"You want us to go out in public tomorrow? Together? After they published this story?" Silas stared at him in wonder and then smiled at him, looking amused. "You've changed more than I thought you had."

"I guess I have, haven't I?" Levi said, matching Silas's grin. There had been a time when Levi had done everything he could to stay out of the public eye. The media scrutiny about Silas and Levi when they'd first started dating had been overwhelming to say the least. Levi hadn't wanted to do anything that made them an easy target for the paparazzi. He supposed after a few years in the limelight on his own he was used to it now. "It'll give them something to talk about anyway."

"You can say that again," Silas said, shaking his head. "I'm in if you are."

Levi gave him a slow smile. "Did I mention the talent show?"

Silas gave him a slow blink. "Talent show?"

"Yep. Frankie is going to sing. You and me? We're back up."

Silas grimaced. "Any chance I can be a front row groupie instead?"

"Nope." Levi quickly texted both Hope and Frankie back, confirming their plans for the next day, and then went to retrieve his guitar. "Ready for a lesson?"

Silas pursed his lips, appearing to be contemplating the question. "What kind of a lesson?"

Levi smirked. "Singing lesson."

"You know I don't sing."

"You do tomorrow." Levi strummed a few chords. "It's just a local talent show. You don't want to let Frankie down, do you?"

Silas rolled his eyes. "I seriously doubt Frankie is expecting me to sing."

Levi held up his phone, showing the text message chain where Frankie had typed in all caps, *SQUEEE!* "She's pretty excited to have not one, but *two* backup singers."

"That's not cool," Silas said, covering his face with his hands. "Not cool at all."

"Come on. It's not that big a deal. You're Silas Ansell, Oscar winning actor. Surely you can learn a few backup verses. Just think, it'll be something new you can add to your résumé."

Silas dropped his hands and sat back into the couch, eyeing Levi with a mischievous look. "How about we make a deal?"

"Uh-oh. Here it comes. What's this going to cost me?" Levi gazed at Silas, feeling more relaxed than he had in ages.

"Singing lessons in exchange for a few hours of working on that scene we have to do on Monday." Silas held Levi's gaze, his eyes full of challenge.

Levi wanted to look away. He wanted to groan or swear or flat out refuse. But he didn't do any of those things. The fact was they did need to work on that scene. And if they did it in private, maybe they'd have half a chance of getting comfortable enough to work through the emotional scene. "It's a deal. Singing lessons in exchange for a rehearsal of Monday's scene."

Silas blinked at him. "That was a lot easier than I expected."

Levi shrugged. "The scene needs work. And even though I think my life would be a thousand time easier if Marcus did replace me, that's not what I want. Plus, I know it's killing you that we failed today. One way or another, we're going to walk onto the set on Monday ready to kill that scene."

"We are?" Silas asked. "You sure about that?"

"Yes," Levi said stubbornly. "We'll work on it as long as it takes until we get it right."

"As long as it takes?" Silas's gaze dropped to Levi's lips and lingered there.

Levi snapped his fingers at the other man. "Focus, Si. We have work to do."

"Work. Right." Silas's eyes crinkled at the edges as he tried to hide a smile. "Which first? The singing lesson or the kiss?"

Levi sucked in a sharp breath and then started to choke, sending Silas nearly into hysterics.

"You should see the look on your face," Silas wheezed as he stood and walked to the door to let Cappy out. "You did realize I meant we'd have to work on that kiss, right?"

Levi finally got himself under control, and then without thinking, he jumped up from the couch and strode over to Silas.

"Levi, what—"

"Shut up, Silas." Without any other warning, Levi pressed both palms to Silas's cheeks and then kissed Silas with everything he had.

CHAPTER 12

*A*ll thought fled Silas's brain. The only thing he could focus on was the fact that Levi was holding him, kissing him as if he was a starving man and Silas was the only one who could fortify him. And Silas never wanted it to end.

Reaching out, Silas buried one hand into Levi's dark curls and clutched his T-shirt with the other, desperate to keep the man as close as possible.

But with Silas's touch, Levi suddenly broke off the kiss and let out a wistful sigh, touching his forehead to Silas's as they stood there just breathing each other in.

"Where did you go?" Silas asked. When Levi didn't answer, Silas stared down at his wet lips and said, "Kiss me again."

"Si, I don't think—"

"Stop thinking, Levi," Silas whispered. "Just let yourself feel."

Levi hesitated for just a moment and then kissed Silas again, this time tenderly, with a reverence that nearly broke Silas's heart all over again.

That was why Silas had fallen in love with Levi. When he

gave himself to someone, he gave all of himself. It was a gift he'd taken for granted and if Levi ever gave him another chance, he wouldn't make that mistake again.

Levi let Silas go and took a couple steps back.

Silas's entire body went cold with the loss of his touch.

"I think that's enough practice," Levi said, his voice husky as his gaze locked on Silas's.

"For now," Silas said.

Levi ignored the statement and reached around to open the door, letting Cappy back in. Then he retreated to the couch where his guitar was waiting for him. "Are you ready for your singing lesson?"

Silas wasn't sure how he was going to sit calmly with Levi when all he wanted to do was taste him again. But he forced himself to sit next to Levi and nod. "I'm ready."

"Okay, good," Levi said softly as he strummed the guitar.

Cappy nuzzled Silas's hand, asking for his ears to be scratched. Silas mindlessly gave the golden retriever the attention he craved and waited for Levi to start.

Then he waited some more.

When it was clear from the mindless strumming that Levi's head wasn't in the game, Silas said, "Levi?"

"Yeah?" Levi abruptly stropped strumming as his head jerked up.

"Everything okay?"

Slowly, Levi shook his head. "I shouldn't have kissed you like that. It was... impulsive and had nothing to do with the scene we have to do on Monday."

"You're right, it didn't," Silas agreed, nodding. "But that doesn't mean you shouldn't have done it."

"Silas," Levi said, sounding exasperated. "We can't just pick up where we left off and act like the past two years never happened."

"That's not what we're doing. At least it's not what I'm doing," Silas said, though he knew that if Levi asked him, he'd dive right back into Levi's arms, hopefully forever. But it was clear Levi didn't want that. "You kissed me because you wanted to. We both wanted it. And we both know we'll never get through filming on Monday if we don't burn off some of the tension between us."

Levi let out a sardonic laugh. "You think *that* burned off some of the tension?"

Silas's lips quirked into a half smile. "No. But it did kill that anticipation of what it was going to be like to kiss you again. Now when we do that scene, I won't be wondering if you want to kiss me as much as I want to kiss you. Because I already have my answer."

"Okaaaaay," Levi said and strummed his guitar again. "I think that's enough talking about that. How about we work on the song Frankie is going to sing tomorrow?"

"Sure. Anything you want." Silas leaned forward, hands clasped, ready for anything Levi wanted to throw at him. Because after all this time, he now knew that Levi wanted him just as much as he wanted Levi. It was then that Silas started to believe that maybe, just maybe, if he played his cards right, they could get their second chance.

They spent the next hour working on Frankie's song. To Silas's surprise, Levi was an excellent teacher. He had a way of coaxing notes out of him that Silas had no idea he could access. By the time Levi put his guitar off to the side, Silas was starting to believe that he could have a future in music if he wanted it.

"What do you think, Levi?" Silas cleared his throat and then belted out the chorus to Harry Styles's latest hit. "Am I giving Harry a run for his money?"

Levi winced and just shook his head as he rose from the couch and headed into the kitchen.

"Come on. It wasn't that bad, was it?" Silas called after him, enjoying the hell out of himself.

"It's so bad that Cappy is hiding under the kitchen table. Give the poor guy's ears a break, will you?" Levi returned with a couple of beers and handed one to Silas. "Do you really want to keep singing, or do you want to do something else?"

That got Silas's attention. "What did you have in mind?"

"Well, I've been working on a new song, but the lyrics aren't quite right. I was wondering if you'd brainstorm with me."

Silas clutched his beer bottle as he sat up straighter, his shoulders back, giving Levi his full attention now. "You want me to help you write a song?"

He shrugged one shoulder. "We could try it. If you're up for it, I mean. No pressure."

"I'm up for it. What's the song about?" Silas was flattered that Levi felt comfortable enough to share his work in progress with him. He knew from experience that writing could be an intensely personal thing and that it took a lot to share work with someone else. Especially unfinished work.

"Let me play it for you." Levi picked up his guitar again and played a couple of chords before quietly singing the song he'd been working on. "When I was with you, time used to be golden, sunrises, sunsets, all of my days and nights wrapped up in you. Now we're older, some say wiser, but I'm moving from coast to coast, living out of hotel rooms. And your name is up in lights, the marquee mocking me with dates I can't make."

The guitar music faded away and Levi put the instrument aside as he tapped a note into his phone. "What do you think?"

Silas was dumbfounded. "It's about us?"

Levi gave him that exasperated look again. "Of course it's about us. Every song I write about a love interest is about us. Didn't you know that?"

"Dammit, Levi," Silas said, pressing his hand to his heart. "Are you trying to kill me?"

"No." Frowning, Levi met Silas's gaze and asked, "Don't you listen to my songs?"

How was Silas supposed to answer that? He knew honesty was the best policy, but how did he tell his ex that it was just too painful to listen to his lyrics?

"You don't, do you?" Levi asked, taking the pressure off Silas.

He shook his head slowly. "It's just... too hard," Silas finally said. "Hearing you singing and knowing you're probably singing about us is a level of torture I'm not prepared to handle."

"Right." Levi got up and started carrying his guitar toward the guest room.

"Where are you going?" Silas called. "I thought we were going to work on your song."

"We were, but now I'm thinking maybe that really is too weird."

"It's not," Silas reassured him. "Trust me. I want to help."

Levi looked uncertain but then eventually sat back down. "Obviously this song is about a long-distance relationship, but I'd rather the focus be on supporting each other instead of the distance tearing these two characters apart. Does that make sense?"

"Sure," Silas said with a nod and tried to ignore the regret in his gut that he always carried with him when it came to his relationship with Levi. "How about something about feeling closer to the person when you see them on the big screen. Like 'When I see you on the big screen, I can't help but smile. Through the distance and the sleepless nights, I know you're waiting. There's nothing at all between us but some long roads and empty miles. Someday, baby, I'll be in your arms again. Until then, when I see you on the big screen, you always make me smile.'"

Levi stared at him, looking dumbfounded. Finally, when he spoke, he asked, "How did you do that?"

"Do what?" Silas asked, genuinely confused.

"Just spit out words like that," Levi said, already picking out chords to go with the new verse. "I've only had that happen a few times and certainly not during my first writing session."

"I'm a natural?" Silas suggested, not at all sure that he'd be able to do that again. It just so happened that he'd lived the life that Levi wanted to capture in the song. It made it easy to brainstorm.

They spent the next few hours drinking beer and putting down suggestions for bridges and hooks. By the time Silas had downed his sixth beer, the room was starting to spin. When he got to his feet, he wobbled a little, needing to hold onto the couch for fear he'd never make it to his bed.

Levi, who'd only finished two beers, jumped up and immediately wrapped an arm around his waist, doing his best to hold him up. "Whoa there, Si. How about we get you to your room?"

"How about we go to your room?" Silas said, giving Levi an exaggerated wink.

"Not tonight, buddy," Levi said gently. "Consent and all that."

"Consent, right. I consent!" Silas declared, holding his hand up in a triumphant gesture.

"I bet you do," Levi said under his breath. "Let's go, man, the bedroom is this way."

Silas followed without complaint, and when he woke up the next day, naked with a pounding headache, he grimaced to himself and wondered aloud exactly how he'd ended up naked.

"I undressed you," Levi said with a shrug.

"And I missed it?" Silas said with a groan. "Dammit!"

CHAPTER 13

"Why do my eyelids feel like sandpaper?" Silas asked as he rolled over with a groan.

"Because you've only slept for about four hours," Levi said, leaning against the doorjamb of Silas's bedroom, amused by the man who was lying on the bed with just a sheet covering his lower half. His naked lower half.

"Four hours?" He squinted toward the window. "It's still dark outside. Why are you doing this to me?"

"You're the one who insisted we not miss that run on the beach. I was set to let you sleep in, but you made me promise to get you up. You said you had to work off the pasta from last night's dinner." Levi supposed he was some sort of masochist for enjoying Silas's pain after the five-thirty a.m. wakeup call. It was Silas's own fault though. Levi really had been planning on letting him sleep off the alcohol until Silas kept insisting.

"Oh, hell." Silas swung his legs over the side of the bed, still clutching the sheet to himself. "Are you just going to stand there all morning, or are you going to let me have some dignity while I get myself dressed?"

Levi snorted. "It's not like I haven't seen it all before. I mean, you're the one who dropped trou last night right in front of me and then tripped and nearly split your head open. It's not like I could just leave you to it after that. I had to make sure you actually made it into bed, didn't I?"

"Just stop," Silas said with a shake of his head. "I don't want to hear any more. Give me ten minutes and I'll be myself again, all right?"

"Sure." Levi glanced down at Cappy, who was leaning against his leg, and added, "Come on, boy. I'll get you breakfast while your dad tries to curb his headache."

"I don't have a headache," Silas said, unable to hold back a wince.

"Sure you don't," Levi replied as he gestured for the dog to follow him into the kitchen.

The sounds of disgruntled muttering filtered from the bedroom, making Levi chuckle to himself. In the past, it had been a rare event when Silas drank that much in one night. In fact, Levi could count on one hand the times he'd actually witnessed Silas even drunk enough to slur his words. The night before had been something else. Entertaining? Yes. But also a little worrisome at the speed Silas had downed his six-pack of beer. It was as if the other man had just been waiting for a moment when he could escape into a beer haze.

After feeding Cappy, Levi busied himself making breakfast smoothies. If they were going to get to the beach for a run, there was no time for a sit-down breakfast. He packed a backpack with water, Ibuprofen, a few power bars, and treats for Cappy.

By the time Silas emerged from his bedroom, dressed in sweats and a T-shirt, Levi had Cappy's travel harness on him and the backpack slung over one shoulder.

"Here. Drink this. You'll feel better," Levi said as he handed him a thermos.

"What is it?"

"Protein smoothie." He handed him two pills. "These are the painkiller chaser you'll be looking for."

"You're a god among men, Levi," Silas said with a grateful smile.

"Are you sure you still want to go running? You look like you could use a couple of hours more sleep."

"Yes, I'm sure," Silas said. "I could use some sea air to clear my head. Plus, Cappy would be disappointed."

Levi glanced over at the dog, who was waiting impatiently by the front door. "You're not wrong," he said with a chuckle. "Okay then, let's go so we can get back in time to pick up Frankie for the farmers' market."

Silas grabbed his smoothie and led the way out the front door and to his car.

Levi waited while Silas got Cappy situated into the back seat and then asked, "Do you want me to drive?"

Silas blew out a breath and handed over the keys without a word.

With his lips twitching with amusement, Levi climbed into the driver's seat of the Tesla. Five minutes later, they were on the highway, headed toward the coast. The moon was still high in the sky, casting a silver reflection off the nearby river. "I've missed this."

"Early morning runs where you make me get up before dawn?" Silas asked.

"I did miss torturing you," Levi conceded. "You always were cute with your bedhead and pillowcase lines embedded in your cheek. But I was talking about the moon shining down on the river."

"All I heard was that you think I'm cute." Silas winked at Levi.

"That is what you'd hear," Levi said, feeling a tingle in his belly. It was strange how his attraction to Silas felt just like it had when they'd first gotten together. The longing and anticipation were a drug Levi couldn't afford to become addicted to again.

They rode in silence for the next few minutes. Finally, Silas reached for the radio and turned it on. The Britney Spears song "Toxic" came on.

Levi glanced at him, turned the volume down, and said, "I finished your script last night."

Silas's head snapped up. "You have my script?"

Frowning, Levi kept his attention on the road and said, "You sent it to me last night. Do you not remember that?"

Silas groaned and covered his face with his hands. "Exactly *how much* did I drink last night?"

"A whole six-pack, plus the wine you had with dinner." Levi navigated through a winding part of the road. "Did you not want me to see it? We can pretend I didn't, but you should know I think it's brilliant."

"You do?" The awe in Silas's voice surprised Levi a bit. Silas had always been confident about his art. Levi had assumed he'd feel the same about his television script.

"How could I not? It's us. At its core anyway. The details are different, but it's our story," Levi said quietly, still thinking about the kiss Silas had written at the end of the season finale. Silas hadn't just written a pilot. He'd written an entire sixteen-episode season.

"You're not mad?" Silas dropped his hands just enough to watch Levi's face.

"Hell no, I'm not mad. I think it's a brilliant coming-of-age story that deserves to come to fruition." Levi's heart was still full after reading through all the episodes. He'd been up half the night, unable to close his browser after he'd started reading the scripts. "Is Shannon shopping it around?"

Silas shook his head and then stared out the window, making it impossible for Levi to read the expression on his face.

"Why not?"

"She doesn't know about it yet."

"Seriously?" Levi was shocked. Silas and Shannon were very close. She was the one person he'd trusted over the years. The one he talked to about everything. Or she had been before Levi had come into his life. "Has anyone else seen the scripts?"

"Just you."

Levi's heart swelled as he realized that Silas, albeit drunk Silas, had shown Levi something that was deeply personal before he'd shared it with anyone else. "Thank you for sending it to me. I love it."

Silas turned in his seat then, giving Levi his full attention. "I was worried you'd be upset."

"You have nothing to worry about. It's not like you told my life story."

The premise of the show was the coming-of-age of two young gay artists who meet at a performing arts school. The Levi character was a dancer who lived with his aunt because his parents were both in prison for running a money-laundering ring. In addition to being criminals, his father hated that his son was a dancer instead of a football star, and his mother did everything she could to coach the gay out of him. His aunt, on the other hand, loved him unconditionally. The fact that she was fighting a long-term battle with cancer meant the character had a lot on his plate and was very guarded about opening up to anyone.

Silas's character was a little more on point. He was a child actor, but instead of having awful parents who pushed him into roles he didn't want, he had taken it upon himself to help his hardworking mother pay the bills. It meant he pushed himself to do whatever it took to get them out of poverty, and his mother let him, often relying on him even when she didn't need to. She was a loving mom who'd gotten used to her son taking care of her. It meant that character had way too much responsibility for a seventeen-year-old and was in a codependent relationship with his only surviving parent.

There were plenty of friends who were side characters with their own stories of course, but the two main characters were versions of Levi and Silas who had to work through many of the same issues and hang-ups as they had in reality over the years. Issues they still were working through.

"I wasn't going to show anyone at all. That's what too much beer will do to a guy, I guess," Silas said, giving him a sardonic smile.

"You weren't? Never?" Levi turned left onto Highway 101, heading toward his favorite beach.

Silas shrugged. "I suppose I didn't think I was ready to show anyone yet."

"You should give it to Shannon. I'm telling you, Si, it's brilliant." Levi felt deeply in his soul that Silas's show deserved to be on air. It was full of complicated family dynamics while being funny and heartwarming and showing young people how important and rewarding it was to invest their energy into found families.

"Maybe I will," he said, running a hand through his hair

before letting out a breath. "Damn, that's frightening. Way worse than acting. This is…"

"Personal?" Levi asked.

"Yeah. Very. When I'm on stage, I'm acting out someone else's vision. This is all me. Sink or swim, you know?"

Levi laughed. "You mean like pouring your heart and soul into a song and then sharing it with the world?"

"Yeah. Like that." Silas's voice was soft as he watched Levi. "I always thought you were braver than I am."

"Seriously?" Levi whipped into a parking space and turned the car off. "You're the one who's been out there in the spotlight all these years, brushing off intrusive fans, ignoring tabloid gossip, and living your life however you see fit. Meanwhile, I'm the one who is always stepping back from the spotlight just to get some peace."

"I wouldn't call going on a world tour and starring in a movie 'stepping back from the spotlight.'"

"You know what I mean. I have to retreat to recharge. Shut everything down and pretend the rest of the world doesn't exist. You just take it in stride, the good and the bad. Have you ever noticed that Seth does most of the interviews for Silver Scars?" he asked, referring to his bandmate. "Even when I am there, Seth does most of the talking. I love singing and creating and that feeling of the energy of the crowd when we're on stage, but the rest of it? It's just draining."

"Yeah, I noticed," Silas said. "Most of the time when I saw you in interviews, I knew you were counting down the minutes until you could retreat to the hotel."

"Exactly. But you… even when you're tired and need a break, you can flip a switch and just be on. Charming and full of graciousness. It's impressive, actually."

Silas reached over and covered Levi's hand with his own.

Levi knew he should pull his hand back. That Silas's touch would bring more than just friendly comfort. He'd been feeling Silas's touch for months after they parted, but he just couldn't bring himself to break the connection. Levi needed this. Wanted it more than he could put into words. Craved it even. After the kiss they'd shared the night before, Levi knew that no matter how bad of an idea it was, if Silas wanted to touch him, kiss him again, Levi would not deny him.

Levi stared down at their hands, wondering what Silas would do if Levi pulled him into his arms.

Silas squeezed Levi's hand. "Thank you."

"For what?" Levi asked, his breath hitching in his throat.

"For believing in me." After caressing the back of Levi's hand with his thumb, Silas quickly pulled his hand away and jumped out of the car. When he opened the back door to free Cappy, he added, "Come on. Daylight's burning. We better get that run in before we have to head back to town."

"Right." Levi took a moment to collect himself before climbing out of the car. He pocketed the key and then followed Silas and Cappy onto the beach. Once they were near the shoreline, they both took off at a slow pace.

An hour later, both of them sweaty and out of breath, Levi dropped to his knees and then fell backward onto the sand.

Silas mimicked him and then laughed when Cappy licked his face.

"He's going to sleep well today," Levi said, still trying to catch his breath.

"I'm more than a little jealous of the nap in his future."

They grinned at each other. Levi sat up, enjoying the stretch and pull of his fatigued muscles. Running was the one time in his day when he could block everything out. Well, except for today. This morning he was all too aware of Silas moving beside him. It had been both a comfort and an annoyance. He just couldn't stop thinking about the man after he'd stripped out of his clothes the night before when Levi had made him go to bed.

Nor had he forgotten the invitation Silas had issued.

'You could sleep right here next to me, Levi,' Silas had said with hooded eyes.

Levi's body had given a full-fledged yes, nearly propelling him right into the bed. But his head had refused. Silas had been drunk. Though Levi hadn't realized just how drunk he'd been, it was clear that Silas had been in no condition to consent. Besides, if Levi ever found his way back into Silas's bed, it wasn't going to be after a drunken night when they were forced to spend time together.

Talk about destructive.

"Silas! Levi! Hey," a voice called from a few feet down the beach.

Silas climbed to his feet, a big smile on his face. "August! What are you doing here?" The pair gave each other a brief hug.

Levi's jaw tightened as he watched the two men embrace. He remembered that Silas had said he and the PA were just friends and even that August was straight, but the familiarity between the two of them made Levi's green-eyed monster rear its ugly head.

"I was paddleboarding when the sun came up." The other man gestured to where his gear had been left on the beach about fifty yards away.

Levi eyed the paddleboard and wetsuit.

"Now I'm just enjoying the morning before I head back into town. You two are here early. What brought you out to the coast?" The man had an easy smile for both of them.

"We just went on a run and are going to head back into town now. Levi's sister is singing in a talent show and we're backup," Silas explained.

"Seriously?" August clapped his hands together, showing his excitement. "The one at the farmers' market?"

Silas nodded.

"You can bet I'm not going to miss that. Levi, I've been dying for a chance to catch one of your concerts. The timing just hasn't worked out. The last time you played in Seattle, I was busy coaching Befana Bay's high school basketball team in the state championships. It killed me to miss the Silver Scars concert, but the girls won, so I can't really complain. Can you imagine little Befana Bay coming home with a state championship title?"

"Impressive," Levi said, just because he knew he had to say something. But all he really wanted to do was drag Silas away and keep him all to himself. It was stupid and petty, but he couldn't help his possessive feelings.

"Very impressive," Silas agreed. "Also impressive to be paddleboarding in the ocean. Do you have water magic or something?"

August nodded. "I do. It makes it easier for sure, but it's not impossible to do even if you don't have that gift. I'd be happy to take you out sometime if you want to try."

"I'm down," Silas said, turning to Levi. "I bet you'd be great at it."

"I don't think—"

"Aww, come on, Levi. I've seen clips of you commanding a stage. No doubt you'd be a natural," August said with more charm than should be legal.

"I think you'd love it. I tried it a few times in Befana Bay,"

Silas said. "The peacefulness on the water is something you'd really enjoy."

Levi had to admit that he had always loved being on the water, and he knew that Silas was onto something. Besides, it meant he had an excuse to spend another day with Silas, even if it meant sharing that time with August. "Yeah. Okay. I'm in."

"Excellent," August said. "Next weekend? Saturday morning?"

"You're on," Silas said.

August clapped Silas on the shoulder and then moved toward his gear he'd left on the beach. "See you both at the talent show," he called over his shoulder as he waved one last time.

Levi gritted his teeth and sat back down to pet Cappy.

"Why don't you like August?" Silas asked, looking at him curiously.

"I never said I didn't like him."

"You're right. You didn't. But don't think I can't tell how you really feel. If you had your way, you'd have teleported him back to Bcfana Bay," he added with a chuckle. "You're still jealous."

"No, I'm not," Levi insisted. "He's straight, right?"

"As far as I know," Silas said.

Levi let out a small snort and then stood. "Come on. We need to get going."

Silas smirked, no doubt having seen right through Levi's lies. Then he stood and clipped Cappy's leash on his harness. As they made their way back to the car, Silas said, "Levi?"

"Yeah?"

"There's nothing to be jealous about." Silas paused and met Levi's gaze. "The truth is, there's only one person I've ever had eyes for. And if I thought there was a chance of getting him back, I'd be all in."

Levi's breath caught in his throat as he stared, dumbfounded, at his ex.

"You weren't expecting me to say that." It was a statement, not a question.

"I guess not," Levi said, wondering if he had the guts to match Silas's honesty.

"You always said the one thing you admired most about me was my willingness to put my heart on the line," Silas said. "That hasn't changed."

Levi could feel the intense emotions radiating from Silas. The love they'd shared was right there, lurking beneath the surface. And even though it terrified him to open the door to their failed relationship, he couldn't stop the words that came straight from his heart. "There's always going to be a chance with us, Silas."

Silas just stared at him, appearing speechless, and then a moment later, he stepped in closer and wrapped his arms around Levi. He paused for just a moment before he leaned in and kissed Levi with such tenderness that Levi knew then and there that no matter what the future held, his heart would always belong to the man holding him in his arms.

CHAPTER 14

*S*ilas never wanted to let Levi go. Now that the man he loved was back in his arms, Silas's heart soared with happiness. The kiss they'd shared the night before had been because they needed to practice a scene. This kiss, though? This was different. This was a promise of what could be. What they'd had in the past and what they could have again.

This right here was everything he needed in life. A good movie to work on. Morning runs on the beach during the sunrise. And his partner by his side.

The problem was, he knew everything that was happening was temporary.

Once the movie wrapped, Levi would go back on tour and Silas would go back on location, doing some movie or TV show. But the chances of them living in the same city and having time for each other were very slim.

That didn't mean he didn't want to try to defy the odds.

He just wondered when he'd mess it all up and let Levi down again.

Reluctantly, Silas pulled away from Levi and said, "I guess we'd better get going."

Levi blinked at him, confusion flashing in his expressive eyes. "Uh, yeah. Probably."

"Right." Silas glanced down at Cappy and said, "Come on, boy. Time to get home."

Cappy took off up the beach, pulling Silas with him.

Levi didn't say anything as he followed them.

Silas slowed until Levi was walking beside him. "So, that happened."

"Yeah," Levi said with a nervous laugh. "I don't know what it means, though."

"Me neither, but I'm not gonna lie and say I don't want it to happen again."

"Si, the physical part of our relationship was never the problem. I think we both know that."

Instead of answering, Silas reached over and entwined his fingers with Levi's just because he needed to touch him. When Levi didn't pull away, Silas tightened his hold, cherishing the moment. It had been far too long since he'd had the luxury to just reach out and touch Levi. If the man beside him didn't object, Silas was going to make the most of it.

But as soon as they reached the parking lot and spotted another couple headed for the beach, as well as a white van that looked suspiciously like a paparazzi vehicle, Levi pulled away and ran a nervous hand through his curls.

"Dammit," Silas muttered and put his head down as he got Cappy into the car. This time Silas climbed into the driver's seat.

As they pulled out of the parking lot, Levi twisted around, watching to see what the van would do. Just as they were nearing a curve in the road, the van shot forward out of the lot and turned east on the highway, following them. Levi turned around and sat back in his seat. "They'll never leave us alone, will they?"

"Not as long as we stay visible in the entertainment industry," Silas said. "Does it bother you that they likely have photos of us on the beach?"

"Yes. Doesn't it bother you?" Levi asked incredulously.

"No." Silas shook his head.

"Why not? What just happened back there is our business. It wasn't meant for public consumption. I just don't understand everyone's fascination with our personal lives. Why can't they just let us figure things out without having to do it under a microscope?"

This was the difference between growing up in the spotlight and coming to fame later in life. Silas didn't ever think much about the press writing about him. He was used to it. He'd been a child star after all. He didn't even really know a life where he'd had privacy from the general public. But he could certainly understand Levi's point of view. The past six months, while he'd been living in Befana Bay, it had been really nice to live his life without being followed by cameras the entire time. With no projects in the works and no relationship to report on, he just hadn't been that interesting. And while he'd been anxious that maybe his time in the spotlight was over, he couldn't deny how nice it was to go to a coffee shop and not have to dodge a gaggle of reporters.

"I get it," Silas said. "I think I've had to endure it so long that the invasion of my privacy is just normalized. I've dealt with it by just ignoring it."

"I can't just ignore them, Silas. Especially when they are making up narratives that aren't true and are damaging my reputation to the point that the execs are telling me if the movie fails, it's *my* fault. What are they going to do with these pictures? What story will they make up next?"

"I imagine they will speculate that we are back together," Silas said, trying to ignore the pinch in his chest.

"What happens when they find out we *aren't* back together?" Levi asked, narrowing his eyes at Silas.

He'd known that was coming. That Levi would voice what Silas had already known to be true. One kiss on the beach along with a declaration that they both still wanted each other didn't mean anything. Their relationship issues were the same as they'd always been. The truth still hurt, though. "Then I guess they'll have to find something else to write about."

"Great. I can't wait."

Silas let out a heavy sigh as he pulled off the road at an overlook. After putting the car in park, he turned to Levi. "I know you don't like the public scrutiny we get when we're together. If there was something I could do to change that, I would. You know that, right?"

Levi grimaced and then squeezed his eyes shut tight before opening them to look at Silas again. "I'm sorry. I know none of this is your fault. I shouldn't be taking it out on you. It's just so infuriating. Not to mention draining. I wish I could just tune them out and pretend they don't exist like you do. But that's really hard when their energy starts to creep into mine."

Reaching up, Silas cupped one of Levi's cheeks. "I know it's harder for you due to your spirit magic. If there's something you need me to do to make it easier on you, just name it."

"There's nothing you can do," Levi said, leaning into Silas's touch as if he craved the connection just as much as Silas did.

"I can lay low," Silas said. "Let you and Frankie have the day together without me. You know they'll be following us now."

Levi covered Silas's hand, holding it lightly. "You can't do that. We're ordered to spend the weekend together, remember? Besides, I don't want them dictating what we can and can't do. Frankie is expecting both of us now. We can't let her down just because of some paparazzi pictures."

"Sure. We can't let down Frankie," Silas said, trying to pull his hand away.

Levi tightened his grip, forcing Silas's hand to stay in place. "I'm also looking forward to singing with you." He smirked and then let go of Silas's hand. "You're not getting out of it that easily."

Silas rolled his eyes. "Fine. I'll do the talent show. But for Frankie, not you." He started the car, but before he could put it into gear, Levi placed a hand on his arm, stopping him.

"I'm sorry," Levi said.

"For what?"

"For freaking out. It's been a long time since the paparazzi has cared what I'm doing on any given day."

Silas raised both eyebrows. "Are you really saying they didn't follow you around while you were on tour, trying to get incriminating shots?"

Levi shook his head. "We had press at all our gigs, so they had access to us already. I suppose if I'd been doing anything besides performing and then disappearing into my hotel room, they'd have found me more interesting. It was never like it is when we're together. Like I said earlier, the media's fascination with our relationship is really baffling to me."

"They publish whatever gets clicks. Face it, Levi, we're just more interesting when we're together." Silas gave him a cheeky smile as he put the Tesla into gear and eased back onto the road.

"They're not wrong," Levi agreed, but then turned to look out the window.

Silas wanted to ask what he meant by that. To clarify once more where they stood, but he kept his mouth shut, already knowing the answer. It was going to take more than a kiss on the beach to fix things between them. Silas just needed patience. And a little luck.

~

"CAPPY!" Shannon called as the golden retriever ran into her backyard.

Silas hesitated at the back door and called, "Are you decent?"

Shannon laughed. "Of course I'm decent. Get your butt out here and give me all the dirt. I'm dying to know how it went with Levi last night."

Levi cleared his throat and slipped past Silas. "Hey, Shan. It's nice to see you again."

"Oh." She covered her mouth as she laughed. "I didn't realize you were here, too."

"Obviously." Levi walked over and gave her a hug.

Silas watched them and was overcome with a wave of nostalgia. How many times had this very scene played out exactly the same way when he and Levi had been together?

"Hey, Silas! What are you doing in there? Get out here," Shannon called.

Silas stepped out onto the patio just in time to catch Cappy jumping into the pool after a fallen leaf. He groaned. "Sorry, sis. I'll get him out."

"Don't worry about it." She waved an unconcerned hand. "The pool needs cleaning later today anyway. Let him have his fun."

Levi had taken a seat next to Shannon and was leaning back

in the chair with his eyes closed, his face tilted toward the sun. He seemed so comfortable. Like he belonged. Silas ached for that to be true again.

"What are you two up to today?" Shannon asked.

"We're headed to a talent show," Levi said, his lips curved into a small smile. "Silas is going to show off his pipes."

"Seriously?" she asked, her voice high-pitched with surprise. "Silas doesn't sing."

"He does now." Levi opened his eyes and met Silas's gaze. "Right, Si?"

"It appears so." Silas took the empty seat next to his sister. "It's just backup for Frankie. Don't go overboard and start adding singing to my résumé."

"We'll see," Shannon said, smirking. "It never hurts to have something else to bargain with."

"Well…" Silas started.

Shannon eyed him, suspicion lurking in her expression. "Spit it out, little bro. It's obvious you have something you're not telling me."

"I've been working on something and want your opinion."

"Okay. You're not going to leave me in suspense, are you?" she asked.

"Check the shared Dropbox," Silas said. "I put a file in there just before we headed over here."

Eyeing her brother with suspicion, Shannon opened the computer sitting on the side table next to her and then clicked on a folder. "This looks like a script."

"It's an entire season of scripts," Levi said. "And they're incredible."

"An entire season?" The disbelief in her tone set Silas on edge.

"Yeah, an entire season," he confirmed. "It's not all that

surprising that I'd write something, is it? I always said I was interested in screenwriting."

"No," Shannon said carefully, but then shook her head. "Actually, yes. It *is* surprising, but only because you didn't say one word about this. There are sixteen scripts in this file!"

Silas shrugged. "I don't tell you everything."

"Or anything by the looks of it," she muttered and cast a quick glance at Levi.

"What's that supposed to mean?" Silas asked, narrowing his eyes at his sister.

"Nothing. Other than the pictures that popped up online this morning," she said dryly. "I mean, I thought as your sister and your manager that I'd know you were back together with Levi before it was published on the most popular gossip site on the internet. But I guess I was wrong," she added, sounding salty.

Levi's eyes popped open as he sat up straight. "What pictures?"

"The ones with you two lip-locked on the beach," she said, tilting her head to the side with attitude.

"Of course," Levi muttered and then got to his feet, starting to pace.

"You two *are* back together, aren't you?" Shannon asked tentatively.

"No," Levi and Silas said at the same time.

Shannon bit down on her bottom lip. "But that photo, it was from today wasn't it?"

Silas nodded.

Levi said nothing.

"Got it." Shannon closed her laptop and got to her feet. "You're not together but were kissing on the beach. How should I spin that when the publications start asking for statements?"

"Don't give a statement," Silas said. "it's no one's business but ours."

"Nothing? Not even a denial?" she clarified.

"Nope." Silas met Levi's gaze and wondered what was going on beneath his blank expression.

"So, no comment. Got it." Shannon glanced between the two men. "Off the record, though, what's really going on?"

Silas just laughed at her. "It's not gonna work, sis. Good try though."

She turned to Levi and got an amused smirk.

"You two. I can't believe you're not giving me the scoop. Me. Your sister."

"Sorry, Shannon," Levi said, his face pinched. "When there's a scoop to be had, I'm sure you'll be the first to know."

"Fiiiine," she whined in an exaggerated tone. "Don't tell me. But the moment whatever this is between the two of you really does become something, I expect a full in-depth report. Got it?"

"A full report? With details? You're dreaming, sis," Silas said, shaking his head at her. "But I'll tell you what; if Levi and I ever have a change in the status of our relationship, I'll send you a text. How's that?"

"A girl has to take what she can get, I guess." She sat back down and opened up her computer. "Now get out of here so I can read these scripts I just found out about. I don't want you here clouding my judgment."

Levi got to his feet and patted her on the back as he walked by. "Do yourself a favor and have the tissues handy. You're going to need them."

Her eyebrows shot straight up to her hairline. "It's a tear-jerker?"

"No." Silas let out an exasperated breath. "It's a coming-of-age dramedy. Levi is just a sap."

Shannon glanced up at Levi. "What are we talking about here? A travel pack of tissue or an entire box?"

"I'd go for the entire box." He bent down, kissed her on the cheek, and said, "It was good to see you again."

"You, too, Levi. Don't be a stranger, okay? Even if my smelly brother isn't around. Come see me. I'll feed you and kick your butt at poker."

He laughed because there was no way anyone was beating him at cards. His spirit magic made it so that he could read people's emotions. And that meant he knew when they were bluffing. It was a terribly useful skill to have. "You can try, but we both know you'll be humiliated."

"Humiliated?" She scoffed. "Oh, ye of little faith. I've got this. Now get out. I apparently have work to do."

"Call me as soon as you're done," Silas told her. "And don't sugarcoat it. If you like it great, but I'm more interested in what you don't like. It'll help me polish it up before you start submitting."

"No holding back. Got it." She waved them off. "Go get Frankie before she thinks you've abandoned her. And Levi, tell Hope hi for me. I'll see you later when you pick up Cappy."

"Will do." Levi grabbed Silas's hand and tugged him gently toward the door.

Silas really wanted to stay rooted to where he was so that he could watch his sister's reaction, but when Levi whispered in his ear that it was time to go, a shiver ran down his spine, making him powerless to do anything other than follow his first love anywhere he wanted to go.

CHAPTER 15

"*F*inally!" Frankie cried as she ran down the stairs. "I thought you two would never get here."

Levi glanced at his watch. "We're five minutes early." Considering their busy morning, the fact that they'd made it on time to pick up Frankie was a minor miracle.

Hope appeared from the kitchen, holding a coffee mug. "She saw that you two went to the beach this morning and was worried you wouldn't make it back in time."

Groaning, Levi rubbed the back of his neck. "I think it should be a rule that no one googles me anymore."

"I didn't!" Frankie insisted. "But my friend from school texted me. Look." She shoved her phone into Levi's face. "Do you think I want to see my brother making out in public? Ewww."

Silas couldn't help the laugh that escaped his lips. Frankie was a handful, and he was here for it. Levi needed someone with fire in his life to keep him on his toes.

"We weren't making out," Levi said, rolling his eyes.

Hope gave them a skeptical look.

"We weren't!" Levi insisted, sounding a lot like Frankie in that moment.

Silas cleared his throat. "We obviously had no idea that photographers were around."

"Obviously," Hope said dryly. "Anyone need coffee?"

"Yes," Silas and Levi said at the same time.

She nodded and walked back into the kitchen. Levi followed with Silas behind him.

Once they were both holding their mugs, Hope looked at Levi and then Silas. "Want to tell me what's going on?"

Levi clamped his lips together and shook his head, unwilling to discuss this with his sister, especially with Silas in the room. What was she thinking?

Silas, on the other hand, didn't have any issues. "We were practicing the payoff scene last night and I think it's fair to say that some old feelings have been brought to the surface. That's all. There's nothing more than that to report."

Levi turned and gave him a what-the-hell look.

Silas just shrugged. "It's the truth, right?"

"Yeah, but..." Levi squeezed his eyes closed and shook his head before turning to face his sister. "Can we not talk about this now?"

"Sure," she said with a soft chuckle. "It's just that I don't get to interrogate you anymore since you're never here. I missed it." She winked and then handed him a brown paper bag. "Coffee cake to go with your cup of joe."

"I both hate and adore you." Levi bent down and kissed her on her cheek. "Are you going to make it to the talent show today?"

"Chad and I will be there with bells on," she said, grinning past him at Frankie, who'd just walked in.

"Please. Nooooo," Frankie whined. "You're too embarrassing."

"I'm embarrassing?" Hope asked, pretending to be offended. "You wound me." She clutched her hand over her heart and acted like she was weak in the knees. "Maybe no bells. Just party favors then."

Frankie rolled her eyes and retreated from the kitchen, muttering something about how old people just didn't understand anything.

Silas let out a bark of laughter. "Never a dull moment with that one."

"You got that right," Hope agreed. "Wouldn't change her for the world, though." She turned to Levi. "Seriously, Chad and I will be there, but we might be a little late. He has a meeting this morning for a new project. We'll come over as soon as he's done."

"What new project?" Levi asked. Chad owned Magical Notes, a music store that was on Main Street.

Hope glanced past him into the living room. When she spotted Frankie, she said, "I'll tell you later when it's just us. I don't want to tell anyone else until we know for sure it's happening."

Whatever it was, Levi immediately understood they didn't want Frankie to know about it yet. "I'm holding you to that."

She gave him a salute and then sent them all on their way.

"What took you guys so long?" Frankie complained on the way to the car. "How long does it take to drink a cup of coffee anyway? I probably have gray hair by now."

Silas abruptly stopped, causing her to run into him. When he turned around, he made a huge show of searching her roots. "Uh-oh. You're not gonna like this."

"What? You actually found gray hair?" Frankie twisted her

head as if she could see anything. Then she reached up to feel the spot he'd been inspecting. "No way. It can't be gray. I'm only thirteen!"

"You must be one of those lucky people who gets an edgy gray streak early in life," he said with a straight face. "If I were you, I'd just go with it. Right, Levi?"

The horror-stricken look on Frankie's face nearly made Levi bust a gut, but he kept it in. And without even cracking a smile, he said, "It's either that, or spend a lot of time and money trying to color it. I hear it's really hard to get gray to take color. It might not be that easy to match this reddish-brown tone you have going on either. Better to just roll with it."

"I do not have gray hair!" she shrieked, pulling out her phone. She opened her camera app and pushed the button so that she could take a selfie. Then she snapped a bunch of pictures so she could inspect her roots.

Silas threw his head back and laughed and then opened the back door of his Tesla for her. "Get in, Frankie. You can search for gray hair while we head to the farmers' market."

The young teenager scowled at him. "I don't see any gray. You're mean."

"Are you sure?" he said, needling her some more.

Frankie turned her big wide eyes on Levi. "Tell him to stop."

"Silas, stop torturing her," Levi said. "It's bad enough that she's already turning gray at the tender age of thirteen."

She narrowed her eyes at her foster brother. "You're evil."

"It's one of my many charms." Levi got into the front passenger seat. When Silas climbed into the driver's seat, they grinned at each other.

"Sure. You two have your fun. I'll get you back when you're least expecting it," Frankie said from the backseat.

"I'd expect nothing less," Levi said. "Just save it for after the talent show, huh?"

She crossed her arms over her chest and stuck her lower lip out. "No promises."

"Fair enough."

The parking lot at the farmers' market was so full, Silas had to park two blocks away.

"Are we going to be late?" Frankie asked for the third time. "We're not going to make it, are we?"

Levi grabbed both his and Frankie's guitars from the trunk of the Tesla and said, "We have plenty of time. Don't worry."

"I think we have to check in. What if they fill up and we don't get a spot?" she asked, walking two paces faster than both Levi and Silas.

"I already signed us up. Our spot is guaranteed. Just try to relax. This is supposed to be fun," Levi said, trying to soothe her nerves.

"I can't." She lifted her shaking hands to her face and shook her head. "I think I might throw up."

"Hey," Silas said, crouching down in front of her. "Look at me. Focus right here."

She opened her fingers so she could peek at him. "I can't do this."

"Sure you can. All it takes is a little courage and a little faith. You've still got both of those, right?" he asked.

She shook her head. "Not right now. I'm the biggest coward that ever lived."

Levi had to hold in his chuckle. Her dramatics were so over the top there was no denying she was made for show business. He just knew that if she wanted it, one day she'd be a huge star.

"Nah. You can't fool me. I can see it," Silas said, his head tilted as if he were studying her eyes. "That bravery, it's right there, pouring out of you. You can't fool me."

Frankie shrugged one shoulder. "I can be brave... when I have to."

"That's right. It's in here." He tapped her chest right over her heart. "You're not going to let something like your silly nerves get the best of you, are you? Don't you want to go up there with me and Levi and show both of us up?"

"I could never show up Levi. He's too good," she said, giving Levi a shy smile. "He's a genius."

"I wouldn't go that far," Levi said, feeling awkward. It was always weird when someone close to him treated him like Levi the Rockstar instead of Levi the normal person.

"I think you're right," Silas said, nodding. "He does have that spirit magic that gives him something special. But me? All I have is air magic. It isn't going to help me sing. So be comforted in knowing that you'll for sure make me sound like an amateur at best. In fact, I might even ask to have my microphone turned down so no one has to hear me when I sing off-key."

Frankie dropped her hands and giggled. "You can't do that. Everyone would notice."

He opened his mouth and let out a note that was so far off-key it made Levi's ears hurt. But his heart was full. Silas was skillfully taking her mind off her performance and putting her at ease. Levi loved him for it.

"Stop!" Frankie put her hand over his mouth. "That's awful."

"See? I told you." He stood again and held out his hand to her. "Stick with me, kid, and you'll sound like an angel sent from heaven."

"Seriously, you *can* sing, can't you?" Frankie asked, looking worried.

Silas made a worried face. "I guess we'll find out."

"Levi!" Frankie rounded on him. "What have you gotten me into?"

Levi laughed. "He can sing. He's just messing with you. You trust me, don't you?"

"No. I don't trust either of you now," she said, flipping her hair over her shoulder and then turning to walk toward the talent show stage.

Silas shared an amused look with Levi before striding to catch up with her.

As Levi listened to her pepper Silas with dozens of questions about the film industry, he was eternally grateful for Silas's patience. He answered everything with honesty and a bit of humor, which kept her from thinking too hard about her upcoming performance.

"So, are you more interested in singing or acting?" Silas asked her.

"Music, but it's good to keep my options open, right?"

He chuckled. "Sure. That's certainly the smart way to think about it. You never know what opportunities will come your way, or when you'll find something else you're passionate about."

"Right? I mean, maybe I'll end up a YouTube star. Be one of those people who films themselves cutting their toenails."

"What? Why?" Levi asked, wondering where the hell that had come from.

"I heard people make bank. I don't know why anyone wants to watch videos of other people's feet, but I'm down," she said with a shrug.

Silas snorted. "Frankie, do you know what a foot fetish is?"

"Oh no," Levi muttered.

"Foot fetish. What do you mean, fetish?" she asked, her eyebrows pinched.

"Good luck with this one," Levi said, waiting to see how Silas was going to handle this.

"A fetish is when someone gets aroused by—"

"Oh no! No, no, no. Nope." Frankie's face turned bright red. "I'm definitely never doing that. Ewwwwww."

Levi slipped his arm around her shoulders and pulled her in for a sideways hug. "The world is a strange place, isn't it, kid?"

"Definitely." She gave an exaggerated shudder.

"Come on," Levi said, tugging her toward the stage. "Let's go give these people a show."

CHAPTER 16

*S*ilas stood on the stage with Levi, each of them flanking Frankie as she sang her heart out while engaging the crowd like a pro. He had no doubt she was going to be a star someday. He just hoped it didn't happen too soon. Every kid deserved time to grow into themself before they dove headfirst into such a public career.

If he had to do it over again, he'd definitely give himself a few more years to be a kid. Not that his mother would have allowed that.

Together, Silas and Levi sang the backup vocals. Silas had to admit that he didn't sound half bad. He wasn't ready to cut a record or anything, but he certainly wasn't embarrassing himself.

The wind started to pick up, making Silas's hair fall into his eyes. As he pushed it back, he noticed Frankie struggling to keep her skirt from flying up. She kept pressing the sides down, but it was obvious she wasn't experienced enough to figure out how to work through the distraction.

Levi cast Silas a worried glance.

Silas mouthed, *I've got this.* Even though he was supposed to be singing with Levi at that moment, Silas took one step forward, his entire focus on Frankie. Then he mentally called up his magic and aimed it at Frankie, asking it to create a sort of barrier around her. Immediately, the air stilled around her and she no longer needed to try to tame her skirt.

As soon as she wasn't distracted by the wind, she was once again one hundred percent engaged with the audience, getting them to wave their hands in the air and sing the popular song back to her.

When Frankie sang her last note, she stepped up the stage and raised her arms to a rousing applause. Silas glanced over at Levi. He looked like a proud papa as he watched her soak in the praise.

"Thank you, Keating Hollow. You're the best!" She carefully replaced the microphone onto the mic stand and then ran into Levi's arms, who picked her up and swung her around. Her shriek of excitement sent a ripple of laughter through the crowd that was followed by more applause.

Frankie gave them one last bow and then let Levi and Silas escort her off the stage. Once they were out of the spotlight, she flung herself into Silas's arms. "Thank you!" She buried her face into his chest, squeezing him with such force he found it a little difficult to breathe.

"You're welcome. I hope they didn't notice my voice cracking," he teased.

"You and Levi were perfect," she muttered into his shirt. "Thank you for saving me."

"I didn't do anything. Everything that happened up there was all you, girl. You were incredible."

She pulled back and looked up at him. "You calmed me down and then you saved me from flashing my goods to the entire crowd. I know you used your magic to fix my wardrobe malfunction."

"That's because he's a great friend," Levi said, staring at Silas, his eyes soft and full of something that looked a lot like love.

Silas stared back, his heart swelling in his chest.

"Uh, okay, Silas. You can let me go now," Frankie said, seemingly oblivious to whatever had just passed between him and her brother.

"Right." He released her and shoved his hands into his pockets.

Frankie took off into the audience, running to Chad and Hope, who were beaming at her, leaving Silas and Levi behind.

"You're incredible," Levi said.

Silas gave him a half smile. "Right back at you."

"Seriously, Si. The way you stepped in to help Frankie, I can't thank you enough. Today was magical for her."

"It was for me, too," Silas admitted.

"Silas! Levi!" a familiar voice called through the crowd.

"August," Levi said, sounding a little bit annoyed.

Silas nudged Levi gently and whispered, "You're jealous."

"No," Levi insisted, but there wasn't any heat behind the denial, making it sound unconvincing.

"He's just a friend. And straight, remember?"

Before Levi could answer, August reached them and said, "You guys were fantastic. I think you should take that trio on the road."

"Thanks, man. But really Frankie stole the show," Silas said and gestured for them to take a seat at a table that had just opened up.

Silas took a seat and August sat next to him, leaving the last seat for Levi.

August turned to Levi. "I knew you were talented, man, but seeing it live was something else."

"Uh, thanks." Levi gave him a forced smile and then turned around to watch the next act.

August turned to Silas and raised both eyebrows in question.

"It's not you," Silas said, shaking his head. Though it sort of was. It just wasn't anything August had done. Levi's issues had to do with whatever was going on between him and Silas. But that was between them, and Silas wasn't going to talk about it with August.

Silas stood. "I'm going to grab some drinks. I'll be right back."

"I'll go with you," August said, jumping up immediately.

"Levi, do you want anything?" Silas asked.

He glanced over at Silas and nodded. "Get me whatever looks good."

"On it." As Silas and August made their way to the concession stand, Silas asked him, "What do you have planned for the rest of the weekend? Knowing you, it's probably something like sky diving."

August laughed. "Actually, I'm working tomorrow."

"You are?"

"Yep. Dealing with all the details that make the week run smoother so we'll be ready when you and Levi walk onto the set Monday morning."

Silas grimaced. "That doesn't leave you much time off."

"Don't worry about me. Once we wrap, I'll have at least three to six months off before my next gig. I'll get a bunch of living in then."

"You don't have something else lined up right away?" The

PAs Silas knew were always working nonstop. "If you need a gig, I'm sure I could contact—"

"No, no. I'm good. I promise. I work for a while and then take time off for a while. When the cash reserves get low, I go back to work. You know that saying, work hard, play hard? I take that seriously. I could have another job lined up immediately, I just choose not to."

"Wow. That's pretty amazing." Silas had never in his life been comfortable with taking time off without knowing he had another job lined up. It wasn't a money issue. It was his anxiety about what would become of his career if he didn't keep himself in the public eye. "You don't worry that jobs will dry up?"

"Nah. If I couldn't get another PA job, I'd just do something else until the right job came along."

"You know," Silas said thoughtfully, "I think I might actually envy you."

August gave him an easy grin. "I've heard that before."

"I bet." Silas stepped up to the counter and ordered two root beer floats. "Anything for you, August?"

"I'll get my own," he said, already pulling his wallet out.

"No way. Consider it a prepayment for the paddleboard lessons."

The PA nodded and put his wallet away. "I do love a good barter. I'll get a chocolate sundae and a bottle of water."

Silas placed the order and paid. A few minutes later, they headed back to the table.

Levi's eyes lit up when he saw the root beer float. Then he shared a private look with Silas. There was no doubt he was thinking about the date they'd gone on and gotten stuck at the top of a Ferris wheel for two hours. They'd ended up making root beer floats in Silas's kitchen, and Levi had declared it the best date they'd ever had.

When Levi turned back around to watch the next performer, Silas took his seat and just to get his mind off that date that was vivid in his memory, he asked August more questions about his life. "What do you do during your time off?"

"A little bit of everything I suppose," he said with a shrug. "Mostly I help my grandmother with any projects around her house. But I also do odd jobs for friends and other family. I also hike, paddleboard, and garden if it's the right season for it."

"That's great," Silas said, but he'd barely heard the other man. He was too busy studying Levi, no doubt looking like a lovesick puppy.

Frankie suddenly appeared right next to Silas. "Did you see that act? There's no way we're going to win now. I can't compete with puppies!"

"Puppies?" Silas asked, snapping out of his Levi trance. "Someone brought puppies?"

"Look!" She pointed to the stage where a line of shih tzus were lined up, basking in the audience's applause. "She commanded them to do all kinds of tricks... through song lyrics. It was brilliant."

Silas hadn't even noticed.

"They were really good," August offered. "But you had the better stage presence."

"How is that possible? Did you see how cute those dogs are?" Frankie insisted.

"They were pretty cute," Levi agreed. "But judging is subjective. We'll just have to wait it out and see which way this goes."

Frankie crossed her arms over her chest and stalked back over to the table where Hope and Chad were relaxing, watching a flutist, which was apparently the last performance.

Levi turned around and said, "So, August, how long have you known Silas?"

August frowned in concentration. "I don't know. A couple of years maybe.

"You live in Befana Bay?"

"Yep. Best place on earth," August confirmed.

"Besides Keating Hollow," Levi said.

August chuckled. "I guess that's up for debate. But I'll hand it to you. Keating Hollow is a special place. If I didn't already love Befana Bay so much, I'd move here in a heartbeat."

"Really? What do you love about it?" Levi asked.

"The question should be what *don't* I love about it." August's lips turned up into a warm smile. "Befana Bay has everything I need. My grandmother, family, community, magic, and a coven that's just as well known for their antics as they are their shenanigans. Nothing goes on in that town without the coven's knowledge. They keep us guessing all the time."

"Guessing about what?" Levi asked.

"Everything," he said, grinning this time. "They're spellcasters, ghost hunters, psychics, and dreamwalkers. Now imagine what kind of trouble that can bring. There was that one time when they summoned my grandfather, only they caught him at the most inopportune time and there he was with the newspaper in one hand and a cigar in the other."

"What's wrong with that?" Levi asked. "What exactly is so special about this coven?"

"Nothing. Except for the fact his drawers were down around his ankles and everyone—and I do mean everyone—

saw his crown jewels. Things like that keep people interested in what is going on in little Befana Bay."

"It sounds like a fun place," Levi said, chuckling to himself.

"It can be," Silas popped in. "But it's not as fun or as lovely as Keating Hollow."

"Oh, no. Those are fighting words," August said. "Nothing is more beautiful than western Washington in the springtime. I'll fight you on this one."

Levi held up his hands in surrender.

Silas got up and gently forced his hands down. "Don't ever surrender this one, Levi. While Washington is beautiful and Befana Bay holds its own magical power source, you're right. Keating Hollow is the best place on earth."

Before August could challenge Silas, Frankie appeared again, this time tugging on Levi's hand. "Come on, Levi. Don't be such a stick-in-the-mud."

"Stick-in-the-mud?" Silas repeated. "Where did you hear that phrase?"

"It doesn't matter. Right now, they're getting ready to announce who the winner of the talent show is. Get up. Come with me so I'm not all alone when they call my name."

"Confident?" Levi asked. "I like that energy."

"I just want to be prepared." She pulled Silas and Levi along with her until they were standing right in front of the stage.

Frankie clasped her hands together as if she were praying and closed her eyes while the announcer called out the winners.

"This year's talent show grand prize goes to... drumroll please..."

Someone tapped their hands on a table, making it sound like drums.

"Okay, that's enough!" the announcer called and then

unfolded the piece of paper in his hands. "Today's winner, by unanimous vote is... Terry Tinkerton and her seven shih tzus. Congrats, Terry. You earned every cent of this check. I mean, training puppies is hard work, right?"

"Right," Frankie muttered right before she started whistling so loud Silas was sure he'd be half deaf in his ear. "Well done, Terry!" Frankie called, seemingly elated that the dog lady won.

"Frankie, you don't have to pretend to not be upset. You know that, right?" Silas asked.

"I'm not upset," she insisted. "Terry and her dogs were amazing. Besides, it's just a local talent show, right? No big deal."

"But, young lady, it's the biggest talent show in three counties," a woman with a large brimmed hat said. "Everyone who wants to break into the industry starts out here. It's how you can make connections."

"I've already got—" She was about to say connections, but the other woman cut her off when she handed her a business card. "Do yourself a favor and call me ASAP."

"Why?" Frankie asked.

"Because I'm the one who can get you gigs. See you around, kid."

When the woman was gone, Levi took the card from Frankie and scowled. He crumpled up the card and tossed it into a nearby garbage bin.

"Why'd you do that?" Frankie cried, trying to lunge after it.

"Stop, Frankie," Levi ordered. "She's not a good agent. That woman will try to sign you and then make you pay fees. She's what we in the industry call a predator. They find young people and prey on their dreams. Then when the client wants out of the contract to try something new, they fight them tooth and nail. So no. I won't let my sister sign with someone like that."

"But what if that was my one shot?" Frankie asked, staring at her feet.

"She is not your one shot," Levi insisted. "Nobody has just one shot at breaking into show business. There are multiple opportunities. You don't need to settle for someone like that. Trust me."

"Where exactly would my shot come from, Levi?" she asked. "It certainly doesn't look like anyone else is interested."

"You do realize I'm a rock star, right?"

She rolled her eyes. "Duh. But that doesn't mean you're going to let me travel with your band or anything."

He let out a bark of laughter. "Probably not, but I do know people in the music industry. When Chad and Hope think you're ready, you can do a demo. I'll pass it around and see what I can do."

"You would?" Her eyes were as wide as saucers. "I thought…" She shook her head and wiped a single tear off her cheek.

"What is it, Frankie? Why are you crying?" he asked gently.

"I thought after that video went viral, you'd never want to help me with my music."

"Forget about that video," Levi said, pulling her into a hug. "I'm always going to want to protect my little sister. I think it's time you get used to it."

She glanced up at him through wet eyelashes and smiled so big, Silas thought she'd pop a dimple.

Silas moved in behind Levi and clapped him on the back. "Will you do the same for me?" he asked, trying to lighten the mood a little. "Shop my demo?"

"No," Levi said and rolled his eyes. "Your voice cracks when you're on stage, remember?"

Frankie giggled and then slipped one hand into each of theirs. "Come on. We have a second-place gift certificate to pick up."

"Gift certificate to what?" Levi asked.

"The farmers' market," she said, heading full speed to the judging table. "Now we can hit up the caramel apple stand and get a couple magical practical jokes. I can't wait to pick up toilet water. I heard it makes people fart all day long."

Silas threw his head back and laughed.

"It's not funny," Levi said.

"Of course it is," Silas insisted. "It's potty humor. Get it?"

Frankie fell out laughing while Levi just shook his head at Silas.

"No magical practical jokes," Levi insisted.

"But—" Silas and Frankie said at the same time.

"Nope." Levi put his hand up, silencing them both. "No jokes. That was the deal, right, Frankie?"

Frankie nodded and then pointed to Chad and Hope.

Levi turned around and spotted them handing out jelly beans and then laughing hysterically when the people who ate them got the highest pitched hiccups he'd ever heard. He just closed his eyes and shook his head in exasperation.

CHAPTER 17

*S*ilas walked through his sister's front door, calling, "Put your clothes on!"

"Uh, is there something I should know about?" Levi asked, cautiously glancing around.

"Shannon and Brian have a habit of getting frisky all over the house. It's best to warn them so we don't end up traumatized by seeing my sister's hoo-ha."

"Did you really just say hoo-ha?" Levi asked with a laugh. "What are you, eight?"

"I am a man who has needed eye bleach more often than you can imagine." Silas placed a hand over his heart and dramatically proclaimed, "Trust me. You don't want to walk in on that."

"Eye bleach?" Brian asked, coming down the stairs. "Seriously?" He stopped at the landing and struck a pose, flexing his biceps and sticking his butt out to show off his glutes. "I work out. You'd think you'd at least appreciate my efforts a little bit."

"Ugh!" Silas covered his face with his hands. "You're my sister's husband. Stop. This is so wrong."

"If it's any consolation, I appreciate your efforts," Levi said, surprising Silas.

Silas glanced back at Levi and spotted his easy smile and laughing eyes. Gods, he'd missed seeing Levi looking so relaxed and happy. "You do realize Shannon has a mean jealous streak, right? I'd be careful flirting with her man."

"Ahh, come on now, Silas." Brian put an arm around Levi's shoulders and pulled him in for the most sideways bro hug Silas had ever witnessed. "Shannon won't mind if I get a little attention from a famous rock star." He glanced down at Levi and said, "She's harmless. Mostly."

Levi laughed and untangled himself from Brian. "It's the mostly part that bothers me."

"Yeah. I can see that." Brian waved toward the hallway. "Shannon and Cappy are in her office. Are you guys staying for dinner? If so, it's probably gonna be frozen pizza since I'm not sure we have anything else."

Silas glanced at Levi. He gave Silas a tiny shrug, indicating he'd be fine with it, but Silas wasn't. He only had about thirty-six more hours of their forced togetherness and selfishly, Silas wanted Levi all to himself. "Nah. Thanks for the offer, but I'm pretty beat after the day we've had. And I'm sure we can find something better than frozen pizza in my fridge."

"Your loss," Brian said as he flexed again and then disappeared into the kitchen.

"Brian hasn't changed," Levi said. "I'm glad Shannon has him. But thanks for getting us out of dinner. All I really want to do is go home, put my feet up, and watch some mindless television."

Silas had a vision of them curled up on the couch together

140

just cuddling. Damn, he'd missed that. "Yeah. No problem. Let's go find Shannon and get Cappy."

The two of them walked down the hall. Silas knocked briefly before opening the door of her office. "Hey, sis—what's wrong?"

Shannon was sitting in her desk chair, tears streaming down her face with a tissue balled in her hand.

Silas hurried over to her and crouched down so that he wasn't towering over her. "What happened?"

"This happened," she said with a half sob, half chuckle as she pointed to her computer screen. "You did this. This is *your* fault."

Frowning, Silas glanced at the screen. "What did I—oh." The script for the series finale he'd written was open in a tab and she'd gotten all the way to the end when the two young men had been sitting on a dock, holding hands and promising to meet back at the art camp the next year. "It's not a sad ending, Shannon."

"No, but it's a tear-jerker," Levi said from behind him. "What happens to Kevin is a gut punch. And then he finds out he's moving across the country when he was going to be thirty minutes from Matthew the entire next year. Plus, Matthew has his own issues. What's going to happen to him now that his grandmother has gone into assisted living and he has to live with his problematic dad? These boys need each other, and you've ripped them apart until the next summer!"

Silas blinked at him. "You do realize it's just a show, right? Eventually, they'll get their true happily ever after."

"It's not just a show," Shannon said through her tears. "It's brilliant. I'm not bias either. I swear. I was just going to read one of the episodes and then dive headfirst into my chores, but once I sat down, I have not moved from this chair. I've read every word. Twice. It's so good, I'm terrified of showing it to anyone without a proper agent to represent you."

"What's wrong with you representing me?" he asked, confused. "You've always done a great job for me before."

She waved an impatient hand. "This is different. It's a script. The standard terms will be different, and I don't know enough to feel confident that I'd be getting you the best deal. I just want to see if I can team up with someone so that I don't get this wrong."

Silas sat heavily in a leather chair. "Do you have someone in mind?"

"I want to call Miranda and get her advice," Shannon said, wiping her eyes one more time.

"That seems like a solid plan," Levi said.

Silas had to agree. "I trust Miranda. I'd love to hear what she has to say."

"Good. Can I send this to her?" Shannon asked her brother.

"Uh, what?" Silas asked, panic setting in. He hadn't been prepared to show his work to anyone yet. Though he supposed if Shannon was going to shop it, certain producers would be reading it.

"Miranda has experience with screenplays. I want to know where she thinks this might fit best. Plus her husband, Gideon, used to be a studio executive. I just really feel like they'd have some good advice for us."

"Right. Of course," Silas said, starting to feel nauseated. Was it the idea of sharing his script or the fact that he'd eaten what was essentially carnival food all day?

"Silas?" Shannon asked, eyeing him carefully.

"Yeah?" He held her gaze, willing himself to act normal.

"Are you okay with this?"

Levi stepped up beside him and placed a reassuring hand

on his shoulder. He didn't say anything; it was just his way of showing support. No doubt he could feel Silas was freaking out. But Levi's touch calmed him, and Silas nodded at his sister. "Yes. I'm good with it. Thank her for me, will you? Let her know how much I appreciate her time and advice."

"Of course." Shannon moved from behind the desk and wrapped her arms around Silas, squeezing him tightly. "I am so proud of you. Do you know that?"

"I've heard that before," he said with a smile. She was the one person in his life he could always count on, and her support meant everything to him.

"Well, it's true." She pulled back, but not before she gave him a kiss on the cheek. "Now get out of here so I can pull myself together before I call Miranda."

"You're calling tonight?" Silas asked. "It's Saturday."

"I'm calling her tonight," Shannon said firmly. "If she's too busy to chat, I'll make an appointment for when she can meet me."

"You're obsessed," Silas said with a chuckle.

"No. I'm really good at my job." She winked at him and then nodded to Levi, who was just standing back, observing their conversation. "Levi, take him home, pour him a drink, and then find a way to keep his mind off this tonight. Can you do that?"

Levi's ears turned a dark shade of pink as he stared at Shannon, his mouth working but no words coming out.

Silas fake-coughed to hide a laugh.

Levi gave him an annoyed glance before turning back to Shannon and clearing his throat. "Yeah. I can handle that." Levi tugged on Silas's hand, pulling him toward the door. "Come on, Cappy. We're headed home."

The golden retriever jumped up from the luxurious dog

bed Shannon kept for him and ran past them, his tail wagging in earnest.

"Goodnight," Shannon called after them.

"Goodnight," Levi and Silas called back in unison.

When they got back to the car, Levi took the keys and hopped into the driver's seat. After Silas got Cappy situated in the back seat, he climbed into the front and looked over at Levi. "Got any ideas for keeping me occupied tonight?"

"Stop flirting with me." Levi put the Tesla in gear and backed out of the driveway.

"You're no fun." Silas made a show of sticking his bottom lip out into an exaggerated pout.

"I'm fun," Levi insisted.

"Not right this moment you aren't. Right now, you're responsible Levi who is often exasperated by me. But soon enough I'll wear you down, and you'll be flirting with me without even realizing it."

"You think so, huh?" Levi asked, his face suddenly expressionless.

"Yep. You won't be able to help it when I put an apron on and start making your favorite cookies."

Levi gaped at him. "You're going to bake?"

"Shirtless," Silas added just for good measure. "That will either get you flirting or leave you speechless. And I'm up for both."

"You're pretty cocky at the moment."

"I can get cockier," Silas said in a husky tone.

"I'm aware," Levi said, shaking his head. "Stop. You're embarrassing Cappy."

Silas twisted to look at his dog, who was sprawled across the back seat sound asleep. "Uh-huh. He looks it."

Levi flicked a glance in the rearview mirror and let out a

surprised huff of laughter. "What did Shannon do? Make him swim laps in the pool?"

"She would if she could. It's more likely she overfed him treats and then took him on a walk around the neighborhood."

"Well, that's mundane," Levi said, turning onto the mountain road that would take them home.

"Very. But it's why he adores her."

"He's not the only one," Levi said, suddenly sounding serious. "I missed seeing her these last couple of years."

Silas eyed him, trying to ignore the ache in his gut. "I'm sure she would've liked to have seen you."

"Sure. I just…" Levi blew out a long breath. "It would've been really hard to go there without you."

When Levi stopped the car in front of Silas's house, Silas placed his hand on Levi's arm and said, "I understand. It's why I rarely came back here." He waved at the house. "It was hard to be here without you."

Levi's voice hitched when he asked, "And now?"

Silas held his gaze. "Now? Now that you're here, it feels like home again."

"Si," Levi breathed, sadness clouding his gorgeous eyes.

"You don't have to say anything," Silas said. "You asked. I decided to be honest. Let's get inside. Cookies are waiting to be baked." He quickly slipped out of the car before he did something stupid like kiss Levi or declare his undying love. After the perfect day they'd had, Silas could see himself doing either.

Levi was the one to free Cappy and chase the dog up the stairs.

Silas followed, taking his time, enjoying the moment. He didn't want to take any more moments with Levi for granted. Soon enough, he'd move back to his rental and it would just be

Silas and Cappy. And while Silas could deal with it, he'd miss Levi even more than he had before. In the few years they'd been apart, it felt like they'd both matured and had relaxed to the point that things between them just felt easier. More considerate. Or maybe that was just because they were both on their best behavior. Silas didn't know, but he was more content spending time with Levi than he had been in a very long time.

"Are you coming?" Levi asked, standing in the doorway.

"Yep." Silas hadn't even realized he'd stopped at the bottom of the stairs.

Levi waited for him, and when Silas got to the door, Levi slipped his hand into his and gently tugged him inside.

Silas glanced down at their clasped hands and back up at Levi. "Is this just another practice run for the movie?"

"Not exactly," Levi said. But instead of elaborating, Levi dropped his hand and moved into the kitchen.

Silas followed, watched him feed Cappy, and then waited while Levi grabbed two beers out of the fridge. Without a word, he turned around and headed for the couch. With the remote in hand, he turned on Netflix and waited for Levi to join him.

CHAPTER 18

L evi took a long swig of his beer and tried to decide what he wanted to say. His thoughts were all over the place. He knew it was a bad idea to start something back up with Silas. He also knew that he'd felt happier and more settled in the last thirty-six hours than he had in forever.

The man sitting beside him was everything he'd ever wanted. Kind, thoughtful, giving, smart, talented, and most of all, loving. Levi craved his company.

But could he handle it when Silas inevitably put his career first and left Levi waiting at some hotel or airport or even this house?

He didn't know. Maybe? Would it be better than missing him all the time because they weren't even talking?

"You're doing a lot of thinking over there," Silas said in his quiet, calm manor.

"I guess I am," Levi agreed.

"Care to share what's on your mind?"

Levi gave him a wry smile. "I'd think that's fairly obvious."

Silas gave him a slow smile. "You're waiting for me to either flirt with you or take my shirt off?"

That got a snort out of Levi.

"Both?" Silas asked. "'Cause that can be arranged."

Leaning back into the cushions, Levi cocked an eyebrow. "While I'm certain I'd enjoy both of those things, maybe we need to talk a bit first?"

Silas leaned back, mirroring Levi's posture, and nodded. "Sure. Let's talk."

Levi knew that was his cue to get out everything he wanted to say, but he just wasn't sure where to start. Finally he just blurted, "Can we try again?"

Silas's eyes widened and then he gave Levi a slow blink. "Try again? You mean get back together?"

Levi nodded, feeling as if he might lose the contents of his stomach if Silas turned him down.

"Just a few days ago, you insisted we would be just friends," Silas said. "Out of curiosity, can I ask what changed?"

"Seriously, Silas?" Levi shot to his feet and started to pace. "You've been here the last two days. You've seen that neither one of us has moved on. It's been two years and we're still pining for each other."

"You've been pining for me?" Silas asked, leaning forward, studying Levi's every movement.

Dammit. Why had he used that phrase? Silas would never let that go. "You're not over me."

Silas's smirk disappeared as he slowly shook his head.

Levi's heart started to beat faster and he moved back to the couch, needing to be closer to Silas. "I never got over you, either."

They stared at each other, neither speaking, but for once, Levi didn't need him to say anything. Silas hadn't been the one who'd wanted to break up in the first place. That was all Levi. "So I know we're working together and all that, but what do you say? Can we try this again?"

Silas moved closer to Levi on the couch so that just their knees were touching. "I am never going to say no to you." He slid his fingers through Levi's, holding on tight as he asked his next question. "What happens when I can't keep my promises to you because of my work?"

Levi sucked in a sharp breath. "I wish I knew the answer to that. I want to say that we'll work through it, but even with all the therapy I've gone through, I think I'm still going to have issues with abandonment. It means we'll probably both have to make some compromises."

"I can do that." Silas cupped Levi's cheek, holding it tenderly. "Do you know how long I've been waiting to hear you say those words? To ask me if I want to try again?"

"Since you saw me doing your dishes two nights ago?" Levi teased.

Silas grinned and then leaned in, kissing him tenderly. "I've missed you."

"I know," Levi said, knowing and accepting the fact that he'd just set himself up to have his heart shattered again. But the truth was, he just couldn't be around Silas and not be with him. Was it better to live for true moments of happiness or to protect oneself from ever being hurt again? He'd been through a lot in his young life. If he knew anything, it was that he could survive. It might almost kill him if he lost Silas again, but he'd get through it.

Somehow.

"Hey," Silas said, turning Levi's face to get a better look at him. "What just happened? You look... well, devastated. Are you sure this is what you want?" Silas's voice was shaky as he added, "That you want me?"

"I'm sure," Levi said quickly, moving in to wrap his arms around him. He pressed his head into Silas's chest. "You're the only one I've ever wanted. You know that. I'm just scared, I guess. If this doesn't work out—"

"It will work out," Silas said forcefully. "It will."

The words sounded good. Too good. And it left Levi with a sinking feeling in his gut that no matter how much they wanted this, they were doomed before they even started.

Desperate to live in the moment, he put that thought out of his mind, grabbed the remote and said, "What do you want to watch?"

"You." Silas tightened his hold on Levi and leaned back into the couch cushions so that Levi was snuggled up on top of him.

Levi pressed his hand over Silas's heart, scrolled through Netflix until he found a cute rom-com featuring two men, and then hit Play. "Have you seen this before?"

"No. I sort of banned rom-coms there for a while. Too… optimistic."

"And now?" Levi glanced up at him, soaking in the moment. Being back in Silas's arms made him feel like he was finally home.

"Now I think it's just about the perfect choice." Silas kissed the top of Levi's head and then for the next two hours, they watched the movie, just holding onto each other.

When the movie ended, Levi shut the television off and chuckled softly when he heard Silas's soft snore. Instead of waking him, he rolled off him and took Cappy out one more time for the night, refilled the water dish, and turned off the lights. He'd intended to wake Silas so that they could move to the bedroom, but when he nudged Silas's shoulder, he didn't even flinch. He was out like a light.

Knowing that Silas sometimes had trouble sleeping, he loathed the idea of waking him from a deep sleep, and instead just crawled back onto the couch and curled up on his chest. Silas muttered something unintelligible in his sleep as he wrapped his arms around Levi, holding him close again. Immediately Silas's breathing evened out, indicating that he'd fallen back into a deep sleep.

Levi pressed a soft kiss to his boyfriend's chest, closed his eyes, and slept better than he had in years.

CHAPTER 19

*S*ilas's eyelids felt like they were glued shut as he tried to blink them open. When he tried to move, his body didn't cooperate and he started to wonder if this was what it felt like when someone started to wake from a coma.

Sunlight stung his eyes, making them water as he blinked rapidly, trying to orient himself. When he spotted the man lying on his chest, the memories from the night before came flooding back.

Levi had asked him for another shot. That had actually happened and hadn't been some crazy fever dream.

Panic started to flood his nervous system. Not because he didn't want to be with Levi, but because he was terrified he'd mess it up again.

Cappy ran over and nudged Silas's arm. Careful to not wake Levi, Silas slid out from under him. Levi shifted and curled up on the pillow but didn't open his eyes.

Good. Silas needed a moment to process.

He silently gestured for Cappy to follow him. While they were outside, he felt his phone buzz in his pocket. He pulled it out and frowned when he saw the time and the caller. It wasn't even eight yet, and Shannon was already calling? Something was off. Otherwise, she'd never call that early on a Sunday.

"What is it?" he said into the phone after hitting Accept.

"You haven't seen the tabloids yet, have you?"

He squeezed his eyes shut, not wanting to think about this right now. "No. How bad is it?"

Shannon let out a heavy sigh. "I don't know yet. But they are trying to sell a storyline that you and Levi are back together and that you're already cheating on him."

"What? How the hell do they know I'm back with Levi? That just happened last night," he blurted without thinking it through.

"You're back together with Levi?" Shannon nearly shrieked into the phone. "For real? Like you talked about it and you're together, together? Not just hooking up while doing the movie?"

"Yes. And we weren't hooking up. Damn, Shannon. How messy would that have been?"

"Not hooking up, just kissing on the beach. I see," she said dryly.

"That's different. We were... You know what? Never mind. That's not important. What I need to know is how they got confirmation that we're back together."

She laughed into the phone. "You can't be serious right now, Silas. You've been in this business for how many years? And you can't figure out that the kiss is all they needed to make the assumption that you're dating again?"

"Oh. Yeah." He ran a hand through his hair and then rubbed at his still tired eyes. "Sorry. I just woke up and am still processing everything. Okay, so they assumed that Levi and I are together. But what's this about me already cheating on him? With whom? How in the world did they come up with that?"

"They have you linked to some PA working on the movie. He's unnamed in the articles, but there's a picture of you two hugging and then one from yesterday that makes it look like you have giant heart eyes for him. The headline reads, *Get You a Man Who Looks at You the Way Silas Ansell Looks at His Mystery Man*. I'm telling you, it's blowing up. Memes are already flooding social media and going viral."

Silas closed his eyes and sucked in a deep breath, focusing on the woodsy scent of the morning air. "This is the last thing we need to deal with right now."

"I know what your answer is going to be, but I still have to ask it," Shannon said carefully.

"Don't bother. It's not true. The PA's name is August. He lives in Befana Bay and I've known him for a few years. He's straight and just a friend. It's tabloid BS. Go ahead and float a statement about him being just a friend."

"And what about Levi? Do you want me to confirm you're dating again?"

Silas hesitated, not sure what to say. On the one hand, he didn't want anyone having to deal with cheating rumors. On the other, he wanted to keep his relationship with Levi to himself for a while. He didn't want to share it with the world. Couldn't they just have some privacy, some time to themselves to understand their relationship before they had to explain it to the world? Besides, Levi should be a part of that conversation. "Don't comment on us just yet. Or say something vague about us enjoying our time making a movie together."

Shannon snorted. "That makes it sound like you're in a friends-with-benefits situation. That won't give you any peace. But don't worry, I get what you're saying and will handle it."

"Thanks, Shan."

"You're welcome. That's what I'm here for. And, Si?"

"Yeah?"

"I'm really happy for you and Levi. Tell him I said I miss him."

Silas felt his lips tug into a tiny smile. "He said the same thing about you last night. I'll tell him. Thanks."

After shoving his phone back into his pocket, Silas threw the ball for Cappy a few times before his dog ran to the back door, demanding to be let in. No doubt, he was more than ready for breakfast. So was Silas. It was then he realized all they'd had for dinner the night before was a bottle of beer. Though after his junk food fest at the talent show, maybe that wasn't such a bad thing.

Twenty minutes later, Levi walked into the kitchen, his curls sticking out in every direction, and sniffed the air before he said, "You are a god among men."

Silas grinned, his heart full. "Bacon has a way of elevating even the most mundane man's status."

"You've got that right." Levi walked over and gave him a soft kiss on the lips. "Good morning."

"Good morning." Silas leaned in, covering Levi's mouth with his own, and kissed him until Levi practically melted into him. The morning's drama faded away, and all that mattered was the man standing in front of him. Silas slipped his hand into Levi's messy curls and deepened the kiss, trying to show him exactly how much he wanted him.

Levi wrapped his arms around Silas and then suddenly jumped back when the grease in the bacon pan popped. He grabbed his arm and hissed. "Ouch!"

"Dammit," Silas muttered and turned the stove off. The bacon was done, he'd just forgotten all about it when Levi had entered the kitchen. "Sorry about that."

"Not your fault," Levi said, moving to the sink to run water over his arm. "I shouldn't have distracted you."

Silas came up behind him, carefully inspecting Levi's arm. "Are you okay?"

"I'm fine." He held his arm up. "Just a surprise. That's all." Levi turned around and spotted the two plates on the counter that were already filled with perfectly scrambled eggs and sourdough toast. "I can't believe you made us breakfast. How long have you been up?"

"Less than an hour." Silas transferred the bacon to the plates and then carried them to the table. "Can you pour the coffee? It should be done now."

"On it." Levi grabbed two mugs and got to business. When he was done, he handed one mug to Silas and took the seat next to him.

Silas took a sip and murmured his appreciation. "It's perfect. Just the right amount of cream. Thanks."

"So is breakfast." Levi scooped a forkful of eggs. "I could get used to this."

"So could I," Silas said, his voice cracking a little as the panic started to set in again. Every time he thought about the future, his nervous system went haywire on him. It was as if he couldn't let himself believe any of this would last. Their relationship was only working at the moment because of their circumstances. Once the movie was done, Silas was certain the problems would set in again. How could they not? Surely Silas would get a job somewhere else on location while Levi would go back on tour. They'd be ships passing in the night, and that was what ultimately doomed them before.

"Hey," Levi said quietly. "Stop thinking so hard."

Silas turned to Levi, his lips pressed into a grim line. "There's something I have to tell you."

Levi put his fork down, giving Silas his full attention. "Okay. Shoot."

No doubt he could feel the angsty energy emoting from Silas. He'd always been good at that. Too good. When Silas and Levi were living in the same house, they communicated very well. Silas knew it was because Levi could sense his emotions, which meant he wasn't afraid to ask what was going on. And since Silas was normally an open book, he'd spill his guts every time. It was actually kind of great because nothing ever really festered for long. With distance between them, things had been different.

"I got a call from Shannon this morning. All the tabloids are running stories about us."

"That was to be expected after yesterday, right?" Levi said, frowning. "We saw the paps, so…"

Silas cleared his throat. "Sure. They're already running stories that we're back together."

He shrugged. "That's fine. It wasn't true then, but it's true now." Levi covered Silas's hand and gave it a tiny squeeze. "It's fine if people know, right?"

"Yes. I guess."

"You guess?" Levi's eyebrows shot straight to his hairline. "Is there some reason why we'd need to keep that a secret? I can't imagine the studio would have a problem with it. If anything, it would help promo, right?"

"Yes. It would." Silas got up and started pacing. "That's part of the problem."

"I'm clearly not understanding something," Levi said,

sounding a little testy. "Why is it a problem if people know we got back together?"

"Because I don't want our relationship up for public consumption, that's why!" Silas gritted his teeth and leaned back against the counter, hating that he was fighting with Levi about this. Why *were* they fighting? Probably because Silas was having trouble articulating why he was upset. "Ugh. Can we start this conversation over?"

"Fine by me. I'm not the one who's agitated."

That wasn't entirely true. Silas could see the small tick in Levi's jaw that indicated he was irritated.

Silas took the seat next to Levi again and turned his chair so he was facing him. "I did this all wrong."

"You mean saying you'd get back together with me and then deciding you don't want the general public to know about it? Is there a reason you're embarrassed for the world to know that?" Levi's outburst was sudden and made Silas flinch. He'd never been that quick to fly off the handle before.

"No. I'm not embarrassed at all. Levi, please, I'm proud to call you my boyfriend. I'm just not crazy about sharing this with the world. With the tabloids. We just made our way back to each other. I wanted to enjoy it. You and me together before we let the outside world comment on it or speculate or try to tear us apart. Is it so much to ask for just a tiny bit of privacy? I know we chose to live our lives in the public eye, but I really just want you all to myself for a little while before the frenzy starts up again."

All of the fight had gone out of Levi, and understanding shone in his gorgeous eyes. "It's not too much to ask," he said and reached for Silas's hand. "I'm sorry I jumped to conclusions. But isn't it too late to keep this relationship of ours under wraps? They've already spotted us together."

"They have, but I told Shannon to dodge questions about us or put out a vague statement. I can tell her to change it if you feel differently." Silas's gut ached at the idea he might have hurt Levi. "I don't want you to feel like I'm hiding you. I'd never do that. It's just that we're so new, and I want to hold onto what we have with both hands and cherish it a while before we let the public chime in on our relationship."

"We can do that," Levi said. "We can definitely do that." He reached up and brushed a lock of Silas's hair out of his eyes. "I would like to just enjoy us for a while, too. I don't really care if people know we're together, though. If we're out in public, I don't want to be looking over my shoulder all the time, making sure we aren't photographed."

"That's fair. I don't mind if people know or assume we're together. I just don't want it to turn into a twenty-four-hour news cycle. If we make a statement about being together again, that's exactly what will happen. We'll be getting requests for interviews, and more and more stories will be written about us. It would be nice if we could navigate our reconciliation without all that pressure."

"Agreed," Levi said with a nod. "I'm completely on board. Together, but keep it close to the vest for now. Sounds doable." He kissed Silas's cheek and then turned his attention to his eggs.

"There's more," Silas said with a grimace.

Levi groaned. "This doesn't sound good."

Instead of explaining, Silas pulled up a news article on his phone and handed it over. "They're running with this.

Levi took his time reading the story. When he was finally done, he put the phone down and said, "You do look like a lovesick fool in that picture. Are you sure you don't have a crush on the straight guy?"

Silas didn't say anything at first, and then he threw his head back and laughed.

"It's not that absurd of a question. I've seen that look on your face before. It's how you used to look at me."

"It's how I look at you now," Silas said, his eyes sparkling with humor. "Do you see where we're sitting in this picture? I'm not looking at August. I'm looking at *you*."

Levi studied the picture one more time. As realization dawned, his lips curved into a sexy little smile. When he put the phone down, he stood and held his hand out to Silas.

"Where are we going?" Silas asked as Levi tugged him out of his chair.

"Your room. I'm going to show you exactly what happens when you look at me like that."

"So no breakfast then?" Silas asked, glancing back at the table where their food sat, mostly uneaten.

"I think what I have planned will more than satisfy your hunger." On the way down the hall, Levi stripped his shirt off, and by the time Silas joined him in his room, all thoughts of breakfast had fled.

CHAPTER 20

"*A*nd cut!" Marcus called.

Levi and Silas were standing together, their foreheads touching. It was the tender moment right after their characters kissed to seal the deal that they were finally together.

Levi grinned at Silas. "I guess this weekend worked after all."

"I'd say we owe Marcus a fruit basket or something," Silas said.

One of the minor characters overheard their conversation and snorted. "Fruit. Definitely appropriate."

Levi glanced over at him to find the guy smiling at them and decided he wasn't being a homophobe. He was just amused. The actor gave Levi two thumbs-up. "Nice scene, guys."

"Thanks," Silas and Levi said together as they finally broke apart.

"Brilliant," Marcus said, clapping as he walked toward them. "Just brilliant. Couldn't have asked for a better performance. Well done. I guess you two can thank me later for ordering you to spend some time together. Looks like it worked out for all of us, huh? Maybe I should have intervened a couple years ago. We might be looking at a celebrity wedding by now."

Levi's face flushed hot. He didn't care if the director knew that he and Silas had gotten back together, but he certainly didn't want to talk about it with him or listen to him take credit for them working it out. Nor did he think it was appropriate for him to bring it up while they were on set with a bunch of their colleagues.

"I'll send your gift basket in the mail," Silas said with an easy smile, making it seem like he was fine with the conversation, but Levi could tell he was uncomfortable. It was the way he was picking at the seam on his jeans. Silas only fidgeted when he wanted out of a conversation.

"My wife loves the cheesecake from Harry and David. Happy wife, happy life, right?" He glanced between the two of them. "I suppose the same could be said for husbands, too, though. We're inclusive around here. Obviously."

"Obviously," Silas said dryly. "It is a movie with two male leads."

"Right. That leads me to my next order of business. Can you two join me in my office for a few minutes? There's something we need to discuss."

Levi frowned, trying to ignore the warning bells going off in his head. He just felt it deep in his gut that whatever Marcus wanted to talk about, Levi wasn't going to like it.

Silas had the same frown, but neither said anything as they followed Marcus into his trailer.

Levi sat next to Silas and waited for the bad news.

At least Marcus wasn't angry this time like he'd been the Friday before. He started off offering them something to drink.

"I'm fine," Levi said, just wanting him to get on with it.

"I could use water," Silas said.

"You got it. Sparkling or flat?"

Levi had to keep from rolling his eyes. When he was on tour, no one ever asked what kind of water you wanted. You got a bottle of whatever was available, and that was if you were lucky. Lots of times you just had to get water from a dressing room sink.

"Flat. No lemon or lime," Silas said.

Marcus got a small bottle from his fridge, handed it to Silas, and then sat down, clasping his hands in front of him. He pasted on a smile and dived right in. "Here's the deal. Your relationship is getting a lot of buzz. Major outlets are picking up and running with what happened this weekend."

Neither Silas nor Levi said anything.

"I'll be straight with you. It's a PR nightmare for the movie," Marcus said, his gaze boring down on Silas. "This cheating rumor needs some serious damage control."

"Shannon already sent out a statement," Silas said. "It's completely false, and the garbage they're printing is unfounded."

Levi leaned in, mirroring the director's posture. "All they have is a photo of two friends hugging. It's not like they were caught going into a hotel room together or something."

"True," Marcus said, nodding his agreement. "But you both know that it's not about facts in Hollywood. It's perception. And right now, the word on the internet is that one of my main stars is cheating on the other one. No one is going to buy into this movie if they think one of the main love interests is screwing around on the other. We need to be able to sell tickets. And do you know what sells tickets?"

"Sex," Silas said in a bored tone.

Marcus smirked. "Yes. But also fantasy. And no one is going to believe you two if your relationship looks messy. Right now, it looks very messy."

"Only because people are printing lies," Levi said. "There's nothing shady going on here."

"That's good to hear." Marcus gave them a patronizing smile. "All I need from you two is an interview or two, setting the record straight."

"No," Silas said. "Our relationship isn't up for public consumption."

Levi cut a glance to him. His boyfriend had a dead-serious expression on his face.

"Now, Silas, I know people don't love talking about their personal lives these days. Fans can be so intrusive, and no one wants to hear other people's opinions about their private lives. But all we're talking about is an interview with *Insiders*. It's as respected as one can get in the entertainment industry. Or if you prefer, a one-on-one with Maggie Hall. It'd be a feel-good piece so that your fans can celebrate your new relationship and get people excited to see you and Levi together again."

"We're not making our relationship public right now," Silas said. "So I'm sorry, but we'll have to decline."

"That's not acceptable," Marcus said, getting to his feet. "You signed a PR clause, which means you have to promote this movie. You will do the interviews."

Levi had had enough. The director was giving off a vibe that was making Levi's skin crawl. Everything about this conversation was inappropriate and invasive. He stood. "I'm sorry, Marcus, but the answer is no. We will not allow you to exploit our relationship just to sell tickets to this movie. We of course will do the PR interviews that are required of us, but we will be dodging any relationship questions. Respectfully, our personal relationship is off-limits and no one's business but ours. If there isn't anything else, then I'd like to get back to my trailer so I can prepare for the next scene."

Marcus's face had started to turn a color that looked a lot like an eggplant. Levi didn't care. Silas had a point. They wanted time to settle into their relationship. A media circus was the last thing they needed.

Silas got to his feet. "Is there anything else you need from us?"

"We'll discuss this after you've had time to think about what this cheating scandal means for your career. No one wants to work with someone who is always bringing bad press, Silas."

"Are you threatening Silas?" Levi asked, not bothering to tamp down the venom in his tone. "What are you going to do, blackball him?" Levi turned to Silas, noted his pale coloring, and had a strong desire to kick Marcus in the balls. The man had hit Silas where it hurt most to get what he wanted. If there was anything that would motivate Silas to do what they wanted, it was to imply he wouldn't get any more work.

"Blackball? What is this, the McCarthy era? No. I'm just stating facts. This is a business, and business means playing the game. We all need to make sacrifices for success. This seems like an easy thing to do to ensure robust ticket sales. You don't want the studio to stop doing same sex movies, do you?"

"The hits just keep on coming, don't they?" Silas asked, looking disgusted. "I will not let my relationship be exploited just for ticket sales. Find another angle to bring in sales."

"Exploited." Marcus scoffed. "Why do you think we cast Levi? It certainly wasn't for his acting chops."

Levi started to feel nauseated. He grabbed his boyfriend's arm and said, "Okay, let's go, Silas. I think we all need to cool off."

"Yeah, you two go cool off. Just tell me where so I can send a photographer!" Marcus called after them.

Silas was so angry he was vibrating with emotion. But he held it in until they were in the privacy of Levi's trailer. "That son of a—"

"Forget him," Levi said, cutting him off. "Marcus is way out of line. He's so far out of line he's in the next county. Just remember, he can't force us to exploit ourselves to promote the movie, even if that was his intention. People will come to see it because they want to see you be brilliant as usual, and they'll want to see how awful I am."

"You're not even in the same universe as awful," Silas said, pulling him into a hug. "When people see you in this movie, they'll be backtracking all their idiotic comments from that video. Mark my words, babe, you'll be the star of the show."

"You're delusional," Levi said but tightened his hold on him, expressing how much he appreciated the vote of confidence. "I'll just be happy not to suck."

Silas chuckled. "Thanks for having my back in that meeting."

"Always." Levi pulled back and gave him a curious look. "Can I ask you something?"

"You can ask me anything."

"Why is it so important to you that we don't talk about our relationship? I know you said you didn't want the media in the middle of us, but you do realize I can handle the media now, right? If this is about trying to protect me, that's not necessary.

I travel all over the world, dealing with press while on tour. I know how it works."

Silas sat down in one of the chairs and let out a tired sigh. "I know you can handle it. This is about me." He looked up at Levi with raw emotion in his eyes. "I'm scared. That's the reason. The last time I got caught up in the media game, I lost you. I prioritized all the wrong things. I just want to put you and our relationship first. I want to protect it."

"You went to that party for a media stunt?" Levi asked, latching onto that one detail. "When you were supposed to meet me here, you stood me up for... what, a photo op?" There was no denying the hurt in his tone. "I thought you were there to meet a director."

"I was, but it was just a rumor that he'd be there. The studio wanted us all photographed to hype the show. I probably could have said no, but you know how important it was to me that the show was a success. I spent a lot of time doing what the studios wanted me to do. This time, I want to do things my way."

Levi stood in front of him, holding out both hands. "I get it. But remember, if you have to play the game a little to get where you want to go, then I think that's what you should do. Just don't stand me up unless it's something really important."

"I won't," Silas promised and then leaned in, kissing Levi again.

"Five minutes!" someone called and knocked loudly on the door.

"Time to work," Levi said, running a hand through his curls just to try to collect himself.

Silas's gaze swept over him. "You do realize that you just messed up your hair, right? They're going to put you back in that chair to make it look *naturally* messy, only it will be styled within an inch of your life."

Levi groaned. He hated the hair and makeup chair. Everything took forever. "You probably should have handcuffed me to keep me from doing that."

Heat flashed in Silas's eyes when he said, "That can definitely be arranged."

Levi gave him a slow smile. "Don't make promises you don't intend to keep." Then he winked and went to find his hairstylist.

CHAPTER 21

"*F*inally," Silas said as he and Levi climbed into his Tesla. "I thought this week would never end."

"Same. Now we have the entire weekend to sit in your hot tub and relax."

Silas laughed. "If only. I have that meeting with Miranda Moon tonight, and we told August we'd go paddleboarding with him tomorrow."

"Why did we do that?" Levi asked, tilting his head back and closing his eyes. "What were we thinking? We need a time machine so I can go back and tell us not to make any plans. Especially with August. Marcus is going to lose his ever-loving mind if we get papped with him."

Levi was right. Marcus was going to have a huge problem with them if any new photos involving August showed up in the tabloids. Despite the denial that Silas was seeing August, a few publications had run with that story and had dug up pictures of Silas and August back when they were filming in Befana Bay. None of the photos showed anything other than the fact that the two guys talked to each other, but that was enough for the tabloids to spin a tale. There was enough speculation that all three of them were being followed nonstop. Silas, Levi, and August.

Silas sped down the street toward Shannon's house. They needed to pick up Cappy, then the weekend could start. "Maybe if they see all three of us together paddleboarding, they'll finally believe that August is just a friend to both of us."

"You think they'll really back down now?" Levi asked. "You're a lot more optimistic than I am. At best, they'll write fan fiction about all three of us."

"Sounds kinda sexy," Silas teased.

"Stop. Next thing you know, we'll find out they bugged the car."

Silas cast him a look of horror. "Bite your tongue."

Levi shrugged. "You're the one who said they'd do anything to get what they want."

He wasn't wrong. The week had been a hellscape of threats and passive-aggressive taunts from Marcus. He was still insisting they needed to do an interview to clear up the gossip. But what more was Silas supposed to say? Shannon and Dawson had already answered multiple calls from publications asking about Silas's relationship status with August. The standard line was that they were just friends, but none of them printed that. They made it sound like Silas was doing something wrong for having a friend while he was living with his ex, Levi Kelley. None of it was false. Or at least not false enough to threaten a lawsuit, but the tabloids knew what they were doing. They were vague enough to cover their bases, but knew how to write copy that had people reading between the lines.

Still, Silas didn't care. They could write whatever they wanted. It didn't change the fact that he and Levi were finally back together and the past week had been magical. He came home every night to Levi and woke up with him in his arms. For Silas, every day was heaven and he tried not to think about the day when they had to part again.

The one thing Marcus hadn't complained about was the acting. Levi and Silas had nailed all their scenes. The one they'd filmed today had ended with the other cast and crew giving them a standing ovation after Levi had delivered an emotional scene with his mother. He'd been in the act of firing her as his manager when she had a heart attack and passed away in his arms. A scene like that would be devastating for anyone, but when the character was supposed to be primarily relieved, it was a delicate balance to make sure the audience didn't hate him. No one should have worried though. Levi had handled it with such nuance and depth that Silas wouldn't have been surprised if he got nominated for awards based just on that scene. He'd been phenomenal.

Once the movie came out, no one was going to care who was dating who. They'd go watch it because it was going to be that *good*. Right?

"What is Shannon doing out on the front porch in her robe?" Levi asked as they approached Silas's sister's house.

"Honestly, she and Brian were probably getting it on in the bushes or something," Silas said.

"In the bushes?" Levi parroted. "No, not even Shannon would risk a tick for a quickie in the outdoors."

"You don't know that," Silas said. "You're not the one who has walked in on them eight trillion times."

"No. Only twice," Levi confirmed. "The first time was a few years ago. I found them in the laundry room enjoying the spin cycle."

Silas cackled. "Oh my gods. Shannon does love that washer."

Levi laughed so hard his eyes watered. As he was brushing away the tears, he added, "The second time was two days ago when I was picking up Cappy."

"Let me guess, in the pool?" Silas asked.

"Nope. Try again," Levi challenged.

"The kitchen counter?"

"No, thank the baby unicorns."

Silas smirked. "Then for sure it was on Shannon's yoga mat. Brian just cannot stay away from her when she gets her stretch on."

"Oh, so close," Levi said dramatically. "It was on the exercise bike."

Silas jerked the Tesla to a stop in his sister's driveway and then turned to Levi. "What did you just say?"

"You heard me."

"But how? And more importantly, why?" Silas demanded. "There is nothing sexy about an exercise bike."

"The tight cycling shorts are sexy," Levi offered.

"Oh, hell," Silas said, somehow sounding both amused and horrified. "What did you do?"

"I ran out of there and then bought stock in eye bleach."

"I still don't understand the physics of sex on an exercise bike," Silas said.

"Do you want to?" Levi asked.

"No." The answer was firm as Silas shook his head. "Just nope. I'm telling you, they should have warnings all over the house. *Guests beware, the owners are sex maniacs.*"

"Silas!" Shannon called, running to the car. "What is taking you two so long?"

"We're talking about the logistics of exercise bike sex," Silas called back through the open window.

"Oh, well, if you need tips, we can talk about it later. Right now, get out of the car. I have news."

Silas turned to Levi and whispered, "Do you think it's good news or bad news?"

"Good news. Look at her. She's glowing."

"That's probably an X-rated exercise bike workout afterglow," Silas deadpanned.

Levi let out a bark of laughter. "You never know."

Shannon pulled the door open and then practically hauled Silas out of the car. "There's already an offer on the table for your television series. A serious one!"

"What?" Silas's entire body went numb with shock. "From who?"

"I'm not sure, but Fallon, the agent Miranda connected us with, just called and said be ready to celebrate!" She grabbed his arm and squeezed. "This is so exciting!"

Silas covered her hand with his and gently removed it, still trying to process. The agent had only had the scripts for less than a week. It was very difficult to believe there was an actual offer on the table. No one moved that fast in the film industry. "You know as well as I do that there's nothing to get excited about until a contract comes in."

"There is one. She's bringing it to dinner." She grinned at him. "I told you this project was special."

Silas turned to Levi, who was standing beside him. When he saw the unmitigated joy in his expression, Silas's eyes blurred as he was overcome with emotion. This was one of the many reasons he loved Levi. There was never any jealousy or petty drama about his success, only pride and unwavering support. Silas reached out and hugged Levi, trying to convey in that one gesture just how much it meant to him to have Levi's support.

Levi held on and whispered, "I'm so proud of you."

Afraid if he talked he'd start crying from all the emotion threatening to overwhelm him, Silas nodded and then stepped back. He willed himself to get it together. When he turned his attention back to his sister, he looked her up and down, taking in her robe, and said, "That's an interesting fashion choice. Are you wearing that so you don't have to take as many clothes off when you get home?"

Shannon rolled her eyes. "Very funny, little brother. There is nothing wrong with having a healthy sex life."

"Of course not," Silas said, suddenly wondering if she thought he was trying to shame her. "I'm just giving you shit. You know that."

Her expression softened. "I do." Then she glanced at Levi. "I hope you two are lucky enough to have just as much fire burning between you."

Levi's face flushed bright red as he met Silas's laughing eyes.

Shannon chuckled softly. "I think I have my answer. Good for you." She turned around and rushed for the door. "Give me two minutes and I'll be ready."

Levi slipped his hand into Silas's and squeezed. "I'm very proud of you, you know."

"This wouldn't be happening without you," Silas said, feeling as if his heart might explode. He'd had a lot of career highs over the years, but this moment was different. He felt... complete.

Levi searched Silas's gaze before responding. "I understand what you're saying. But you need to know that this is all you. Your hard work and talent got you to this point. And I'm so

RETURN OF THE WITCH

happy that our stories were an inspiration, but make no mistake, this isn't a one and done for you. If you want to keep creating television series or move into movies, you have the talent and drive to do it. And honestly, I can't wait to see where you go from here."

Those emotions Silas had been holding in finally overwhelmed him and he couldn't stop the single tear that fell down his cheek. "I love you. You know that, right?"

"Yes."

"Good. Now kiss me," Silas demanded.

Levi grinned at him and then moved in for the kiss just as the unmistakable click of a camera went off.

They both froze. Without even looking around to see which photographer was stalking them, Silas grabbed Levi's hand and said, "Let's get inside."

Levi followed without comment and then laughed when Silas pushed the door open calling, "Put the sex toys away. Your little brother is here."

Brian appeared from somewhere in the back of the house. "Perfect timing. I just put the dildos back in the kitchen drawer."

Levi let out an awkward chuckle. "You know, it's pretty funny that I have no idea if you're serious or not."

Brian just shrugged. "I guess you'll have to be careful when you're looking for a corkscrew."

Silas laughed. "Stop, Brian. He thinks you're serious."

Brian raised an eyebrow. "What makes you think I'm not?"

"Oh hell," Silas muttered just as Shannon appeared, wearing a crisp white suit and matching stilettos. "You look incredible, sis."

"It's all the sex," she teased. "It makes me glow."

"Okay. Enough of this conversation. You're making *me* uncomfortable now," Silas said.

Brian cackled while Shannon looked pleased with herself. She said, "Mission accomplished. Let's go. We have a deal to make."

CHAPTER 22

"*S*ilas, it's an honor to meet you," Fallon Featherstone said as she beamed up at him. "I can't tell you how excited I am about your project."

"Thank you. That means a lot to me," Silas said, shaking her hand. They were waiting outside Woodlines, a restaurant on Main Street, while their table was being prepared.

Levi stood back, watching the agent fawn all over his boyfriend and was both amused and also a little uneasy. He wasn't sure why. It wasn't Fallon's energy. She seemed sincere. No, it was Silas's. He was nervous and hesitant, which was normal for this type of situation, Levi supposed. But it was unusual for Silas. Usually he was very confident and sure of himself when around other industry people.

Fallon turned to Levi. "I'm a huge fan. Love that song 'Secrets in my Scars.' Really moving."

"Thanks," Levi said, feeling awkward. Would he ever get used to the praise people heaped on him for his art? He always wondered what he was supposed to say when someone complimented one of his songs. They were so personal when he wrote them that he rarely talked about them, and when he did, he was always vague. It was better to let people connect to the lyrics through their own lens instead of his.

"I'm looking forward to a time when I can see you on tour," she added as she took her seat at the table. "Any idea when you'll be back on the road again?"

"Nothing to report yet," he said. "After the movie wraps up, Seth and I will figure out our next moves."

"Makes sense. It's very exciting. So much is happening for you two."

"Yeah, it's busy. But Silas is the one with the exciting news. I'm sure he can't wait to hear the details about the offer to produce his TV series," he said, trying to end the conversation about his music. They were here for Silas, not his band, Silver Scars.

"Ah, yes. The exciting news," she said, turning her attention to Silas and Shannon. "I have the contract details right here." She patted her messenger bag. "I think you're going to be really pleased."

"I'm here. I made it," Miranda Moon said as she strode up to them, wearing a long, romantic black dress with lace-up boots. Levi loved that she always took her witchy style to the next level. As a paranormal romance writer, she really leaned into that side of her persona.

"Miranda, hi," Fallon said, kissing her on the cheek. "It's good to see you."

Silas and Shannon had asked Miranda if she'd join them. The author and screenwriter had recent experience in navigating deals with studios, and they wanted her to take a look at the offer.

"You too." She squeezed Fallon's hands before turning to Silas and giving him a big hug. "Congrats, baby. I have a really good feeling about this." It was well known that Miranda had a knack for just knowing things sometimes, so it was no surprise to Levi when Silas started to relax a little.

Good. Levi wanted Silas to enjoy this moment. He deserved it.

The door opened and the hostess waved them in and took them to a private table near the rear of the restaurant. They ordered drinks and a few appetizers and then set the menus aside.

Fallon pulled out a legal pad and put a pair of black-framed glasses on. With her blond hair tied up in a neat bun, she was all business. "Let's get into it. I'll start with the fact that this is probably the best contract I've ever seen for a script. And certainly a surprise since it's from Salish Sea Studios."

"It is?" Silas and Levi said at the same time. That was the same studio they were working with to film their movie.

"It is. They seem to love Silas." She grinned and quickly went through the details, highlighting the substantial advance, the production credits, and the options clause.

"That actually sounds pretty decent," Shannon said, reading the email on her phone. Fallon had forwarded the contract to her so she could read through it herself.

"It is. And the studio is eager to snatch it up. Their preempt to keep it from going to auction is substantial," Fallon said.

"What about control?" Silas asked. "Would I, as the creator, get to keep creative control?"

This was the sticking point. Levi could tell by the tension streaming from Silas. He was worried if he just took the deal, they'd change too much of the story.

Fallon frowned. "It's incredibly rare for a studio to give creative control to an untested writer."

"But I'm not just some newbie writer off the street. I've

been working in the industry practically my entire life," Silas said. "I know how the industry works. I know what goes into making a series."

"Yes, I know. But Silas, this deal is a really, really good one. If you take it and the series is a hit, you'll be able to write your own ticket for any new deal down the line," Fallon explained.

Miranda frowned. "I'm with Silas on this one. He should maintain control. Look what happened to my IP the first time I sold it. They changed the most important part of the story. I was furious for years."

Fallon nodded. "Yes. There is always that. I'll definitely bring that up in the negotiations and see what I can do. If they are this eager to get the rights, then they might be open to it."

"They'll do it," Miranda said confidently.

Everyone turned to stare at the novelist.

She flashed a coy smile. "Trust me."

Fallon laughed. "Okay, I will. Let the games begin!"

The waitress arrived, delivering them all their drinks.

"Perfect timing," Fallon said as she raised her wine glass. "To spirited and hardball negotiations."

They all toasted, and after Miranda took a sip of her cocktail, she leaned into Silas. "You know, I'm jealous I can't be a part of this. It's such a great project. I can't wait to see it on my screen."

"Thank you," Silas said and then met Levi's gaze. There was happiness there, but Levi couldn't shake the feeling that something was still off with Silas.

Levi frowned at him and mouthed, *What's wrong?*

Silas shook his head and mouthed back, *Later.*

Despite Silas's clear hesitation, the evening turned out to be a nice celebration and by the time they left, Silas was grinning from ear to ear.

"When did Fallon think she'd hear something back from the studio?" Levi asked after they'd dropped off Shannon and collected Cappy.

"She doesn't know. If they are desperate to avoid a bidding war, she thinks fairly soon. If not, it could be weeks." He sat back in the passenger seat and closed his eyes. "It seems really surreal, you know?"

"How so?" Levi asked, guiding the car up the side of the mountain. Since Silas had been celebrating the interest in his series, Levi had decided to be the designated driver.

"Just the idea that I'll sell the rights to my project. It's been this thing that's been all mine for a long time now, and I guess I'm having trust issues. I've seen too much to believe that they won't wreck it or twist it into something else completely." He sighed. "I know I'm being precious about this. I just can't seem to separate myself from it."

"It's okay to be precious about something you care about so deeply," Levi said. "I feel that way about the songs I write. Luckily, I do get to keep complete control. I don't know how I'd handle it if the execs came through and rewrote my lyrics and tried to tell me that's what I had to sing."

"Thanks for that. I'm trying to use my business head, but when it comes to this project, I guess I'm just all heart."

Levi parked the car in front of Silas's house and turned to him. "It's okay to be protective of your project. Remember that."

"How did I do this life without you for even a few days?" Silas asked.

The love radiating off him threatened to overwhelm Levi. He reached out, brushing his fingertips over Silas's lips. "I have no idea. I wasn't a fan of it myself."

Silas took Levi's hand and kissed his palm. "Promise me we

won't end up separated again. This is the life I want. The one with you in it."

Levi didn't want to make any promises they might not be able to keep. With their careers, the odds were against them. At the same time, he agreed with Silas. He wanted a life with him in it. "I promise we'll always try to work it out. Whatever it is."

"Same."

Headlights flashed from the end of the driveway.

Levi glanced back, spotted the white van, and let out a curse. "Paparazzi again."

They hurried out of the car and into the house. The minute the door closed, Silas pulled out his phone and dialed. "Shannon, there are photographers in front of my house." He paused a second. "Okay. Thanks." He ended the call. "She's calling the sheriff's office now. They should be by soon to run this guy off."

"Do you think this will ever end?" Levi asked.

"Probably not until the hype of the movie is over," Silas said.

Levi flopped down on the couch. "It's pretty clear we're dating. What do they want? A photo of us ripping each other's clothes off?"

Silas snorted. "I bet they'd pay millions for that."

"Ugh. You're right." Levi cast a glance at the window. The shades had been down for days due to high-powered lenses and unscrupulous photographers. "At least we're in this together."

Silas sat beside him and leaned his head on Levi's shoulder. "I wouldn't have it any other way."

CHAPTER 23

"*A*ction!" Marcus called.

Levi dug deep to get into his character's persona. River Ramon was at odds with his management over tour dates and appearances and they were having a meeting. Ezra had already moved back to Seattle, and River was frustrated that they wouldn't be able to see each other for at least another month.

"I'm here," Levi said, striding into the office. "What's the issue now? I already told you I can't do those interviews or that festival at the end of the month. I have plans I can't break."

"You can and you will," the music executive said, slapping a manila envelope in front of him. "Your contract obligates you. If you don't, we'll call in the lawyers."

Levi ignored the envelope. "You can't force me to be your workhorse. Are you really going to sue me for breach of contract over a five-day weekend? You know you won't win."

"No. We're going to sue you over that album you owe us. It was due six months ago."

"Are you effing kidding me? We agreed to put that on hold so I could do that movie you wanted me to do."

"Did we?" the executive asked innocently. "Do we have that in writing anywhere?"

Levi scowled. "So you're going to sue me to do what? Make sure I get it out faster? What's the issue? Are profits down or something?"

"On the contrary. You're our highest grossing artist, and we need you to do that press junket to promote this upcoming album that isn't done and do the festival that we've already committed to."

"I never signed on to do that festival. I told you I'm going to see Ezra." Levi crossed his arms over his chest and glared at them.

"Fine. Be prepared for late fees and penalties for every day the album is overdue. Either deal with the lawyers or just go to Austin and handle business."

The coldness of the studio exec made Levi fume with rage. He'd heard stories of this kind of thing happening in the industry from Silas, but hadn't ever really understood just how hard it was to fight with the studio and music execs when they were armed with teams and teams of lawyers. Because this was a movie, the writers could write it any way they wanted and still end up with a happy ending. But in real life? Who could really fight this? If this was actually happening to Levi, he'd have to cancel his plans and do what they said, no matter how burned out he was. But since River Ramon was fictional, he could do whatever he wanted.

Levi stood, glared down at the actor portraying the studio executive, and said, "Unleash whoever you want. We're done here." Then he walked out, never looking back. In the script, it turned out that his manager had dirt on the executive and no lawsuit ever comes to pass. Later, when the last album is done, River cuts ties and goes with another label who gives him total creative freedom and the right to do whatever shows or press he wants to. He even has the right to do no promo at all if that's what he wants.

It was a fairytale ending that rarely, if ever, happened in real life.

"Cut! That's a wrap for today," Marcus said and then strode off without saying a word to anyone. He'd been icing out Silas and Levi for the past week. That was fine with Levi. He didn't have anything to say to the man who wanted to exploit him and Silas anyway.

"Good job, Levi," August said as he handed him a bottle of water. "Is that it for you? Are you done filming?"

"I think so. I have to be available if they want to redo anything, but as far as I know, I'm free."

"Excellent. I know Silas has a few more days. After that we should all get together and try paddleboarding again, but this time up in Befana Bay. The witches there have a spell to conceal the bay so the paparazzi can't bother the stars who come through town."

"I'd like that." The Saturday they'd planned to head back to the beach with August had gone south quickly when they'd been followed by not one but three SUVs. They'd abandoned their plans pretty quickly and headed back to Keating Hollow, where Silas and Levi had stayed holed up in Silas's house. While it was no fun to be stalked day and night, it hadn't been too much of a burden for Levi to have alone time with Silas. After being apart for so long, he welcomed the privacy of their love nest. Soon enough they'd have to part ways to deal with their own careers. For now, Levi was just going to enjoy their time and try not to worry about the future.

He walked into his trailer and found his phone buzzing with a call. Seth's name flashed on the screen.

"Hey, man! What's up?" Levi said into the phone. Seth was his partner in his band, Silver Scars. He hadn't spoken to him in weeks.

Seth chuckled softly. "I think that's what I should be asking you. Looks like you and Silas are causing all kinds of internet trouble."

"Ugh, don't remind me." Levi sat heavily in one of the chairs. "Why can't we make paparazzi illegal?"

"Because too many stars rely on them for publicity. You do realize you're one of the very few who doesn't actually like to be in the headlines, right?"

"You don't either," Levi shot back. It was part of the reason they got along so well. Neither loved the drama that usually came along with fame and money. All they wanted to do was write songs and play gigs. So far, it'd been working for them. Or at least it had until Levi impulsively decided to star in a movie with Silas.

"True. But there are exceptions. Opportunities that one just can't pass up."

Levi's warning bells went off. Seth was calling with news, not just to catch up on the tabloid gossip. That sinking pit in his stomach was back. "What is it, Seth? Does your old band want you back or something?"

"What? Hell no. Where'd you get that idea?"

"I don't know. I think I'm just extra jumpy lately due to the media frenzy. I'm just waiting for something terrible to go wrong."

"You mean like something with you and Silas? How back together are you? Is this just a movie fling and then you'll go your separate ways, or are you going to try again for the long haul?" Seth asked, his voice full of concern. He knew how important Silas had been to Levi, and he'd been there through the breakup to see just how hard Levi had taken it.

"We're completely back together. In it for the long haul," Levi said, knowing in his heart that was true.

"Wow. I hope it works out for you, brother," Seth said, sounding a little wistful.

"It better, or else you're going to have a mess of a bandmate on your hands," Levi said with a sardonic chuckle.

"Let's not put that energy out there," Seth said and then cleared his throat. "On that note, there's a reason I called. *Rolling Stone* wants us... for the cover."

"Seriously? For real this time?" They'd been contacted before, but at the last minute they'd been bumped when the mega-group Mystic came out of retirement.

"For real this time. They want an in-depth interview with both of us. It's going to be for the December issue. The label wants us to release a single at the same time. So not only do we need to do the interview and a photoshoot, we need to get working on our next song."

December wasn't that far away. Certainly, the magazine would want to get on that as soon as possible, which meant he'd probably have to fly out to New York. The very idea of leaving his bubble with Silas made Levi's anxiety spike. But he couldn't say no. The coveted spot on the cover of *Rolling Stone* was not something someone turned down. Especially when he had a bandmate to consider. "Okay. Let me know when they want to meet. I should be finished up here early next week."

"Have you been working on any songs while you've been filming?" Seth asked.

"A couple. I'll send what I have. You?"

Seth groaned. "Not really. Everything I've gotten down

lately just seems like a worse version of something I've already written."

"It sucks when that happens. Don't worry. We'll get together and make some magic."

"Thanks, Levi. I'll get back in touch soon."

After Levi ended the call, he pulled up a couple of voice notes of the song he'd been working on and sent them to Seth. He knew Seth would listen and play around with them a little before sending them back. Then they'd go from there.

The door swung open and Marcus walked in without even knocking.

"Is there a problem?" Levi asked him. "Am I needed back on set?"

"We're done shooting for today." Marcus took a seat across from Levi. "I just wanted to talk."

The energy streaming off the director was toxic, and it made Levi's skin crawl. He wanted more than anything to get up and leave, but he didn't just in case he still had to work with the man. "What did you want to talk about?"

"This." He pulled a stack of papers from inside his jacket and set them on the table in front of Levi.

Levi glanced at them and noted the top one was a printout of one of the many online articles. This one was speculating that Levi, Silas, and August were a throuple. He gritted his teeth. There was a reason why famous people were told not to google themselves. "There's nothing either Silas or I can do to stop those kinds of rumors, and you know it."

"You can give an interview, and in five minutes all this speculation will stop," he said. "The narrative will turn to everyone wanting to watch you two falling in love on film instead of this trash."

"You don't know that," Levi said, narrowing his eyes at the

man. He could feel an undercurrent of deceit but had no idea what the director was up to. "Too much exposure will just bring more and more interest. It's not going to stop anything."

"You'll control the narrative. Plus it will turn this movie into a blockbuster. What's the problem with that?"

Ah, so that was it. Marcus thought that if Levi and Silas went on a media tour about their relationship, it would turn the movie he directed into a huge success. He didn't really care about the trash tabloids. He was trying to further his own career. Levi stood. "We're not doing it. We'll do the press junkets when it's time to promote the movie, but not this." He moved toward the door but stopped when Marcus grabbed him by the arm. Levi stared down at the man's hand and in an icy tone said, "Let go."

Marcus casually dropped Levi's arm and retorted in an equally icy tone, "You'll regret this decision."

"I doubt it." Levi reached for the door handle.

"You will when Silas's project gets buried." The man sneered at Levi and then brushed him aside on his way out the door. He paused and glanced back. "Think about what's more important, Levi. Success or your precious privacy." Then he stalked off, muttering about ungrateful actors and their entitlement.

CHAPTER 24

*S*ilas had just finished feeding Cappy when the front door opened and Levi walked in, looking slightly windblown and cute as hell with his cheeks rosy from the cool autumn evening. "Hey, gorgeous," Silas said. "Are you up for a night out?"

Levi's eyebrows shot up. "You want to go out? And be hounded by photographers?"

"Don't sound so horrified. I've got a plan to help us stay out of the public eye." He guided Levi toward the bedroom. "Go on. Get cleaned up. Our reservation is in thirty minutes."

"Silas, I don't—"

"Nope." Silas pressed two fingers to his lips, cutting him off. "I'm tired of hiding away, and I want to take you out on a proper date. If you've got other plans or are otherwise engaged, let me know, but I've gone through a little bit of trouble to set this up. Will you indulge me and let me spoil you for an evening?"

Levi nodded once.

"Good." Silas leaned in and kissed him softly. "Now go. Daylight's burning."

Ten minutes later, they were in a black SUV driven by Candy Pelsh, a friend of Levi's who worked at Incantation Café. "You two look amazing," she said as she glanced back in the rearview mirror.

"Thanks, Candy," Levi said, smiling at Silas.

"Oh, you two are so cute! Can I just tell you how happy I am you're back together? If there were ever two people who were meant for each other, it's you guys," she gushed.

Silas reached over and took Levi's hand. "I couldn't agree more."

Levi peered out the back of the SUV. "You do know we're being followed by a couple of photographers, right?"

"Not to worry," Candy said. "They can follow for now, but they won't be allowed access to our destination."

"Where are we headed, the moon?" Levi joked.

"Maybe," Candy said with a cheeky grin. "Just sit back and relax. We've got this handled."

"Who's we?" Levi asked.

Silas just grabbed his hand and held it in both of his. "Keating Hollow's little elves. Now just enjoy."

Levi let out a huff of irritation but had a soft smile on his face, so Silas knew he wasn't actually mad. Just mildly frustrated that he didn't know what was going on. "I got a call today."

"A good call or a bad call?" Silas asked, frowning. Lately all calls Levi had gotten had been from his agent to tell him all about the ridiculous stories that were going around and asking how he should respond. Levi had been a hard no on all of it.

"A good one. It was Seth. He said *Rolling Stone* wants us for the cover of the December issue."

"Seriously?" Silas asked, grinning. "That's a huge deal, Levi. Why didn't you tell me right away?"

"You kind of didn't give me a chance."

"True. Well, now we actually have something to celebrate. Too bad we don't have any champagne." He was kicking himself for overlooking that detail. Though it wasn't exactly legal to drive around with an open container, so it was just as well that they waited until they got to their destination.

"I'm probably going to have to go to New York for the interview and cover shoot," Levi said.

"I love New York. When do we go?"

Levi blinked at him. "You want to go with me?"

Silas gave him a questioning look. "You don't want me to?"

"Of course I want you to." Levi's eyes lit with happiness. "It's just that we were never able to travel with each other before, and I just assumed that you probably already had other commitments."

That felt like a bit of a gut punch, but only because it was true. When they'd been together before, Silas's schedule had been insane. Every time he made plans to travel with Levi, he'd been pulled away by a meeting, or his own interviews, or other press he was obligated to do. Once he'd even taken a last-minute role on an extremely popular television series that ended up turning into a semi-recurring role. No wonder they hadn't made it. Levi must have felt like a complete afterthought. "I don't have any roles booked after this movie, Levi. The only thing I have going on are the script negotiations. I can always do those over the phone. Shannon can go in my place. My calendar is blissfully free. I'd love to go and be your plus-one."

That was a first. When Silas admitted he didn't have any jobs lined up, he didn't feel that crippling anxiety like he used to. He wasn't even anxious for Shannon to find him his next project. When had that changed? *Why* had that changed? Was it because of the man sitting next to him or because of the interest in his television series? He wasn't sure. All he knew was that for the first time in forever, he was content. He felt complete instead of trying to fill something inside of himself.

It was strange but really, really good.

"My plus-one, huh?" Levi beamed at him. "I can't wait."

"Oh. Em. Gee!" Candy cried from the front seat. "Can you two get any cuter? I swear, my heart is about to burst. Where do I find someone to be my plus-one? I have got to get myself a Silas. Stat."

"Not a Levi?" Silas asked, clearly amused.

"Oh hell, no. Levi is like my brother. I couldn't imagine dating him. You on the other hand… sexy, talented, tall, dark and handsome. What's not to like? And don't get me wrong, I don't want to sound like a gold digger or anything, but the car and the house? Both are a real turn on."

"Candy," Levi admonished. "Stop."

"Don't pretend you don't love Silas's house," Candy said with more than a little bit of attitude. "You once told me you couldn't imagine living anywhere else."

"Sure, because it's where Silas lived."

Candy snorted. "No, you said it was for the wide windows and the hardwood floors. But I'll accept that you liked having Silas there, too."

Levi's face was flushed again, but he didn't correct her.

And Silas loved it. He couldn't help pressing his palms to his man's cheeks. "You like me for my hardwood?"

Candy snickered. "He likes that, too."

"If we weren't speeding down the street, I'd pray for the earth to open up and swallow me right now," Levi said through his laughter. "But if my prayers came true, I fear I'd have a wicked case of road rash."

"Can't have that." Silas tugged him closer and put his arm around him. "It's okay if you're dating me for my house. At least I know where I stand."

"Stop," Levi said mildly. "Don't listen to Candy. She's just a troublemaker."

"A troublemaker who has helped orchestrate a magical night out on the town," she said with an air of authority. The SUV turned down a private path that was lined with trees all covered in twinkle lights.

"This is the Townsend property," Levi said, glancing around.

"Yep," Silas said. "It's also cloaked in magic, so even those high-powered lenses won't be able to capture us tonight."

"Seriously? Who cast that spell?" Levi asked.

"It was a joint effort," Candy explained as she came to a stop in front of the Townsends' large log cabin-style home.

"Ready?" Silas asked Levi.

"I have no idea," he replied.

"Fair enough." Silas climbed out of the car and then waited for Levi to join him. With his arm around Levi's waist, he guided him around the house and into the backyard, where the entire Townsend clan was gathered along with every person in Keating Hollow that Levi loved.

The chatter died down as soon as Silas and Levi were spotted. A cheer went up and congratulations were offered by everyone.

Levi just stood there, taking it all in, and then he turned to Silas with pure panic on his face. "What is this?"

"What do you mean?" Silas frowned. "It's a party."

"I mean, what kind of party?" Levi whispered in a shaky

voice. "It's not some surprise where you ask me something, and put me on the spot is it?"

Silas's eyes went wide as he realized what was making Levi freak out. "Gods, no," he rushed out. "I would never do that to you. This is just a party to see all our friends since we've basically been hiding out the entire time we've been here filming. I thought it would be fun to see everyone."

The tension visibly drained from Levi's shoulders as he let out a long breath. "Thank the gods."

"But just so I'm clear," Silas said, trying to ignore the knot of dread in his gut, "marriage isn't for you?"

Levi jerked his head so that he was staring Silas in the eyes. "That's not what I said."

"You just don't want the proposal to be in front of everyone you know?" Silas hadn't been thinking about marriage. Not yet anyway, but now that they were on the topic, he desperately wanted to know where his partner stood. Because there was no doubt that Silas had envisioned them married in the future.

"Well, there's that, but also it's way too early to be thinking about that, don't you agree?" There was no mistaking Levi's uncertainty regarding the topic. "I'm not saying I don't ever want to get married or that I wouldn't want to marry you," he stammered on. "I just... oh hell. I'm flustered."

"I can tell," Silas said, pulling him into his arms. "It's okay, Levi. You're right. It's way too early, and I would never ask you in front of an audience. When or if we decide marriage is for us, we'll decide together, in private, away from cell phones and cameras and electronics of any kind."

Levi gazed up at him, relief rolling off him in waves. "Yeah. That sounds perfect."

"Silas! Levi!" Frankie called as she ran up to them. "Finally. I thought you'd never get here."

Levi gave her a hug and then slipped his arm around her shoulders. "How are you doing, kid?"

"I'm not a kid," she said primly, clearly annoyed.

"That's right. You're a teenager," Silas said.

She nodded sagely and then went to him, hugging him around the torso. "You're my favorite now."

"Score!" Silas pumped his fist in the air. "My work here is done."

Frankie giggled.

"My apologies," Levi said. "But you know, you are my little sister, so I reserve the right to think of you as a kid from now until forevermore. Brother's privilege."

"Well," she said, side-eyeing him, "when you put it like that, I guess it's okay."

Levi winked at her. "Now, tell me everything you have going on. How's the singing going? Are you still working on it? Have you lined up any more gigs so Silas and I can cheer you on from the front row?"

She scoffed. "Please. You are and will forever be my sexy backup singers. I'm making plans for choreography as we speak."

"Choreo. Things are getting serious," Levi said to Silas.

"I'm out. No hip jerking or gyrating for me. I'm too old for that. I might break something."

They were all laughing when Chad and Hope arrived, hand in hand, beaming at them.

Hope gave her brother a hug and asked, "Did Frankie tell you our news?"

"News? What news?" Levi asked.

"I was going to but then we got off topic," Frankie explained, beaming at Chad and looking like he'd just given her the moon.

"Ahh, that's a no, then." Chad waved toward an empty table. "Let's go sit down and I'll tell you all about it."

"I can't wait to hear this. Are we getting a little one?" Silas asked. "Hope, are you preggers?"

"Silas!" Hope cried. "Goodness, no. I have way too much going on for that."

He chuckled, enjoying needling Hope. He knew she didn't plan on having biological children. Her plan was to foster and adopt to grow their family.

"Stop with those thoughts," Hope said, pointing a finger at him. "I don't need that kind of energy right now."

Levi chuckled. "You better use some sage to clear the air, Silas. She's serious."

"Let me check my pockets for a sage stick," he said and then made a show of going through all of them, only to come up empty.

"Don't tease me, Silas. I bet Abby has one around here somewhere," she said and then got up and headed toward the table where Abby was sitting with her husband, Clay.

Chad shook his head. "Now you've done it."

"Okay, why is she so concerned about an accidental pregnancy?" Levi asked. "I mean, I know it's not the plan, but that's pretty over the top, isn't it?"

"Chad is opening a music venue," Frankie blurted.

"You are? Where?" Levi asked.

"Here in Keating Hollow. It's at the end of Main Street in an old warehouse that just came up for sale a few weeks ago," Chad explained. "We have a lot of people taking music lessons these days at the shop, but not a lot of places for people to play live and show off their talents unless they head into Eureka. So we're opening a pub, planning an all-ages day one day a week and having live music, open mic nights, and karaoke the other nights."

"Wow," Silas said, looking at Frankie. "Does this mean you'll be a regular on all-ages day?"

"Yes." Frankie nodded vigorously. "I'll let you know the schedule so you can put it on your calendar. We'll practice two nights a week."

Silas threw his head back and laughed. "You sure know how to work it, kid... er, Frankie. I'll check with my manager and get back to you. Do you pay the going rate?"

"If the going rate is a meet-and-greet with me, then yes." She flashed them all a self-satisfied smile.

"Okay, Ms. Diva," Levi said, ruffling her hair. "Try not to let all the fame go to your head," he added dryly.

"I won't be like that," she shot back quickly. "I'm just messing with Silas. If I'm ever famous, I want to be like you. You're always so kind to your fans. I'll never act too good for them."

Silas watched as they shared another hug and then scanned the crowd to look for his sister. Shannon and Brian were supposed to already be there, but if one of them got handsy while they were getting dressed, who knew when the horndogs would show up. He was just about to give up looking for her when he spotted them entering the backyard, both of them snickering behind their hands and looking like guilty teenagers.

He placed his hands on his hips and waited for them to see him.

"Busted," Shannon said with a giggle.

Silas rolled his eyes. "Do you two ever take a break?"

"Nah. Why would we do that?" Brian asked, clasping a hand

on his brother-in-law's shoulder. "The day I stop wanting your sister is the day you put me out to pasture, got it?"

Shannon blew him a kiss as he strode off to talk to Chad.

Silas shook his head at her. "You can't even be on time for the party?"

She slipped her arm through his and said, "Get a grip, Si. We aren't having sex twenty-four-seven. We were just messing with you. I was late because I got a call from Fallon. She has an updated offer from Salish Sea. She said they gave you everything you asked for, except they lowered the advance and added the difference to the back end. They said if they were going to take a chance on giving you creative control, then you were going to have to prove yourself with receipts. How do you feel about that?"

Silas was frozen with shock. Had he just heard her correctly? Was the studio really going to give him creative control? All of the unease he'd had about selling the project lifted, and he felt like a huge weight was off his shoulders.

"Si?" she prompted.

"Yeah, Shannon. Yes. Absolutely yes." Silas was starting to feel downright giddy. "I don't even care about the advance. As long as the back-end deal isn't just a way to screw me out of the profits, then I'm in. All the way in."

Shannon's eyes sparkled with pure happiness. "I'm having the lawyer go over the contract. It will be thoroughly vetted before I let you sign it."

He nodded and then grabbed her and hugged her. Hard. "Have I ever told you how much I appreciate you?" he whispered.

"Yes," she whispered back. "I only want the best for you."

He pulled back, holding her by her shoulders. "I know. Never once have you made this job about how much *you* make.

You always, *always* default to what is best for me. Do you know how rare that is?"

"You forget I grew up with our parents, too, Silas," she said with a sad smile. "I've seen it all, unfortunately. It's my pleasure to do everything I can to make the best of your career. It also helps that what's best for your career is often what's best for my bank account. Mom really screwed the pooch on that one, didn't she?"

"It sure looks like it." His mother, the ultimate stage mother, had booked him any job that was offered. The faster the paycheck the better. She didn't care if it furthered his career or if he was interested in the job; she only wanted to keep the checks flowing. Once he'd moved to Keating Hollow, he'd cut ties with her and Shannon had been handling his affairs ever since. He firmly believed he wouldn't have the career he'd built without her.

He squeezed his sister's hand. "You're priceless, Shan."

"I know." She hip-checked him. "Let's go tell Levi the good news."

CHAPTER 25

*W*hile Levi loved that Silas had arranged a party for them to spend time with friends and family, he was having a problem shaking off his troubled mood. He'd planned to come home and tell Silas all about the meeting he'd had with Marcus, but he'd been distracted by the date. He could have told him in the car, but he didn't want to talk about drama with the director in front of Candy. Sure, she was a friend, and one he trusted, but he'd been in the business long enough to know that things like that rarely stayed private when the gossip mill started running. All it would take was for Candy to tell one person she trusted and so on.

No, he had to tell him in private where they wouldn't be overheard. The last thing they needed was more tabloid rumors, especially one about trouble between the two stars and the director. If anything would doom a film, it would be that.

"Levi, I want you to meet someone," Chad said.

He glanced up to see a gorgeous woman with wavy, golden-brown hair standing beside his brother-in-law. Levi got to his feet and held his hand out.

"Harlow Thane, I'd like you to meet my brother-in-law, Levi Kelley," Chad said.

"It's nice to meet you, Levi." Harlow shook his hand. "I've got to say, it's pretty exciting to meet one of the singers of my favorite band."

"That's really nice of you to say," Levi said, shoving his hands into the pockets of his jeans as he studied the woman. There was something really familiar about her. "Are you sure we're meeting for the first time? I feel like I know you from somewhere."

"She used to host that show, *Paranormal in a Small Town*," Chad said.

"Right," Levi said, nodding. "Now I see it. You're a medium, right?"

Harlow nodded, looking slightly uncomfortable. Her energy matched her stance, and Levi decided her past wasn't something she was excited to talk about.

For her sake, Levi quickly changed the subject. "What brings you to Keating Hollow?"

"She's going to manage the pub for us," Chad explained.

"That's right," she said with a nod. "After I got out of the ghost hunting-for-hire business, I worked at my grandmother's pub over in Eureka for a while until she sold it. I was at loose ends until I saw Chad's ad for a manager. And now, here I am." She gave Levi a forced smile, making him wonder what was really going on with her.

"Sounds like it was great timing for both of you. Is your grandmother still in Eureka?" Levi asked. "It's nice having family nearby."

"It would be, but she picked up and moved to Arizona. She

said she was ready for pickleball and sunshine 350 days a year."
Harlow's energy changed completely when she talked about
her grandmother. It was light and full of joy. Interesting.

"I bet she's loving it," Levi said.

"She is. Thanks for asking about her."

Levi felt Silas coming up behind him and smiled when his
boyfriend's hand landed on his shoulder. "Hey," he said,
glancing back with a soft smile. "Where have you been?"

"Talking with Shannon." Silas leaned over and kissed Levi
on the cheek. Levi wrapped his arm around Silas's waist and
then introduced him to Harlow.

"Welcome to Keating Hollow," Silas said. "I can't wait to see
what you and Chad cook up with this new pub."

"I'm pretty excited about it myself," she said. "Also looking
forward to that movie you two are working on. I've heard
some really great things about it."

Levi and Silas shared a confused glance, and then they both
laughed.

"What? Did I say something wrong?" She frowned. "I'm
sorry if I overstepped."

"You didn't," Levi rushed to assure her. "Don't mind us.
There's just been a lot of media surrounding us lately that has
nothing to do with the movie, so we were unaware of any
possible press."

"Oh, no. I didn't read it in the press. I have a friend who
works on the set. Carrie Mason. She—"

"Does hair," Levi finished for her. "She's been the one who
has kept my mass of curls under control these past weeks."

"Yes. She mentioned something like that." Harlow rocked
back on her heels. "She said you two really turned it out and as
long as editing doesn't mess it up, it's going to be the romance
of the season."

"That's encouraging," Silas said. "Though I'd say we already have the romance of the season." He winked at Levi.

Harlow glanced between them and then in a soft voice said, "Wow. She wasn't wrong about you two either."

"What did she say about us?" Silas asked curiously.

"Just that the tabloid stuff was garbage and she was pretty sure you two are the real deal."

"We are," Levi confirmed. "Tell Carrie she's a genius. I've never had my hair behave quite as well as when she worked her magic."

"I will," Harlow said.

Shannon suddenly appeared. "Silas, Levi, I don't mean to steal you away, but Hope is looking for you."

They said their goodbyes to Harlow and followed Shannon across the backyard.

"Did you tell Levi the news?" Shannon asked.

"News?" Levi asked. "What news?"

"I haven't had time yet, Shannon. Hold onto your panties." Silas paused and turned so that he was facing Levi. "The studio agreed to my terms. I'm getting everything I wanted. As soon as the lawyer goes over it with a fine-tooth comb, I'm signing. I get to keep my creative rights, Levi. Can you believe it?"

Tears stung Levi's eyes. He was so happy for Silas. He could feel the sense of peace surrounding him and that was all he'd ever wanted for the man he loved. He threw his arms around Silas, hugging him tightly. "I am so, so proud of you. Congratulations."

Silas gathered Levi close, just holding him, and Levi never wanted the moment to end.

"What do you think about scoring the movie?" Silas asked.

Levi pulled back, more than a little surprised. "Seriously?

Why? I mean, you haven't even started, and you're already thinking about who you want to write the music?"

"Remember that song we worked on together?"

"Yeah."

"I keep hearing it as the opening credits," Silas said. "I know it's way too early to really be thinking about such details, but I wanted to lock you down before you released it into the wild."

Levi laughed. "Sure. I'll save that one for your project. It is just about perfect, isn't it?"

"It is," Silas agreed.

"My goddess. Could you two get any sweeter? My stomach aches from all the sap I just ingested," Shannon said with an exaggerated eye roll while unable to hide her amusement. "I mean, people just aren't supposed to be that loving and supportive, are they? You guys are setting a bad precedent."

"Shut it, Shan. Your teasing isn't shaming us," Silas said. "Didn't you say Hope was looking for us?"

"She is. Come on."

They followed Shannon to where Hope was sitting with all of the Townsend sisters and Hanna Pelsh-Silver.

"There you are," Hope said, jumping up and rushing over to them. "Listen guys, I know this night is supposed to be low-key, but everyone is asking if Frankie will sing, and she's a little nervous. I thought if she had her backup singers, maybe she'd feel better about it?"

"I'm in," Silas said immediately.

Levi shook his head at him, and even though he was touched that his boyfriend was so willing to help Frankie, he couldn't help saying, "You're such a pushover. What is she going to do when we're not around?"

"She'll figure it out," Silas said. "But right now, she has us, so let's go give her the support she needs."

"Aww," the Townsend sisters said in unison.

"You're going to be the best brother-in-law," Abby Townsend said to Silas.

"That's my goal." He flashed his trademark charming smile at all the women and then made a beeline to the makeshift stage where Frankie was standing off to the side, looking a little miserable.

Levi jogged to catch up to them.

When Frankie spotted them, her entire face lit up. "You're going to do it? Sing with me?"

"Backup only," Levi clarified. "You need to build confidence if you're going to do a weekly gig at the new pub."

She nodded, looking sober.

Levi wanted to wrap her up in a long hug and tell her it was all going to be fine. That she'd survive getting up in front of a crowd, and that soon enough, she'd have no use for him and Silas. But tonight, she looked terrified.

"What's holding you back, Frankie?" he asked her.

"Everyone who matters is here tonight," she said. "If I mess it up, no one will come to Chad's pub."

Ahh, that made sense. "I hear you. I've been there numerous times. All you can do is try your best. If you're even half as good as you were at the talent show, they'll be blown away."

"You don't know that," she said, glancing nervously at the crowd.

"Yes, I do," he said. "You trust me, right?"

She nodded.

"Okay then. If you mess up so badly that you can't continue, just give the mic to Silas."

"Me?" Silas asked, horrified. "Why me?"

"Because you'll make Frankie look really good," Levi said with a smirk.

Silas groaned. "I hate when you're right."

Frankie was finally smiling. "I wouldn't do that to you, Silas. But thanks for the offer. Let's go. We have a song to sing."

From the moment Frankie got on stage, she oozed stage presence and sounded incredible, just as Levi had known she would. There was only one mishap, and that was when Silas sang off-key and nearly tripped over his mic cord. But even then, Frankie covered for him, and when she was done with her last note, all of their friends and family gave her a standing ovation.

CHAPTER 26

"*A*re you ready to go?" Silas called from the kitchen. "We're going to miss our flight."

"I'm coming," Levi called. "Just trying to stuff my jacket into my luggage."

Silas walked into the living room and found Levi sitting on his suitcase, trying to stuff his puffy jacket into the already overflowing case. "Let me handle it."

"You don't need—"

"I've got room. I'm not the one who's being photographed in eight different outfits." Silas took the jacket and easily stuffed it into his roller bag. "There. Now are we ready?"

"Just one more minute." Levi rushed back to the bedroom, and Silas was starting to wonder if he was going to try to pack the furniture next.

Filming had ended a week ago, and the only thing left to do for the film was promo. They weren't needed for that until about a month before the release, which would be in the spring. Now they were headed to New York for Levi's *Rolling Stone* interview. Silas was excited to be going on a trip with

Levi. While the paparazzi had slowed down on following them everywhere now that August had left town, they were still stalking them. Silas hoped that in New York they could get a little peace. He doubted they'd cause much of a stir in the big city.

Silas chuckled at that thought.

"What's so funny?" Levi asked, adding a carry-on bag to their pile of luggage.

"Me, thinking we'll get some peace in New York City. Imagine having to go to a city of eight million people to get some privacy."

Levi laughed. "Okay. You're right. That is funny. But the last few times I was there, no one cared at all. I think the paps have bigger fish to fry in the city."

"Let's hope so." Silas picked up two of their suitcases and carried them outside. Just after he tucked them into the trunk, his phone buzzed. "Hey, Shan. What's up? Is Cappy okay?" They'd dropped Cappy off the night before. He was staying with her while they were out of town.

"He's fine. Listen, I got a call from the studio today. They are pushing to finalize this contract. They want you on a flight to Los Angeles, ASAP."

"Today? I can't go to LA today. We're leaving for New York." Silas's lawyer had given a thumbs-up on the contract last week. Shannon had let them know it was a done deal, and they said they'd get in touch with a time when they could all meet up. "Tell them to set something up for when I get back. Surely they can wait eight days to ink the deal."

"I tried that," she said with a heavy sigh. "But the producer who wants the IP is leaving for a month tomorrow. They want to lock this down before he leaves the country. Something about protecting their investment, even though they haven't paid you a cent yet."

"They'll just have to wait a month then," Silas insisted as he watched Levi haul his carry-on toward the car. "I'm not going to bail on Levi. Not this time," he added to make sure she got the point.

"Listen, Silas, I understand where you're coming from, but are you sure you want to do this? It's playing with fire. You know how studios are. If we don't sign today and it gets pushed out, there's always a chance they'll change their mind. Especially as they get closer to the end of the year. If some bean counter starts getting nervous about year-end, all projects will be halted. There's never any way to predict which ones will survive and which won't. You can bet your ass that yours would never see the light of day in that situation."

Silas was silent as he took all that in. He certainly didn't want to kill the deal of a lifetime with the studio, but he also wasn't going to stand up Levi. Not this time. Not again. "I can't today, Shannon," he said again. "Can't they send a notary or something to where I am? Do I have to be there in the office to sign the paperwork?"

"For a deal like this? Yes, Si. You need to be there. If you start acting like a diva before the show even gets off the ground, they'll never greenlight it. Can you just meet Levi in New York tomorrow?"

"Is she talking about the deal for your TV series?" Levi asked him, his brows pinched with concern.

"Hold on, Shannon," he said into the phone. Then he answered Levi. "Yes. They want me in LA today to sign the paperwork. I told her no. We have plans, and then that industry party tonight. I won't miss that performance. I've been dying to see you live for the past two and a half years."

DEANNA CHASE

"Are they rescheduling?" Levi pressed.

"I don't know. Apparently, the producer who is handling the option is headed out of town tomorrow for at least a month. And Shannon is worried they'll get cold feet if we wait too long."

"Silas," Levi said, using his stern voice, "get on a plane to LA and go sign that contract. You can meet me in New York when you're done."

Silas just shook his head, his business brain and his heart warring with each other. He desperately wanted to seal the deal for his television series, but his heart was telling him he needed to be in New York. These days he was trying his best to listen to his heart. "This week is about you. We made plans. You're singing tonight. I want to be there."

"I can sing for you anytime." There was no denying Levi was exasperated now. "Go to LA. Stop being stubborn. I promise, I will be fine." He took Silas's free hand in his and said, "*We* will be fine. It's okay."

"Then why is everything inside of me screaming for me to get on that plane with you?" Silas asked.

Levi's expression softened. "Because we have history and you love me enough to not make the same mistakes. But you're not the only one who's grown since then. This deal is important to you. Very important. Which means it's important to me, too. You can't miss it just because we have plans. I want you to be happy. And making this television series is what fulfills you. That's important. Change your flight, get the deal made, and meet me in New York tomorrow. We'll still have time to take that carriage ride in Central Park."

"Why are you so good to me?" Silas asked, feeling like his heart might explode.

"Because I love you." Levi pointed at the phone still

clutched in Silas's hand. "Now tell Shannon you're on your way."

"Thank you!" Shannon shouted so that Levi could hear her.

"You're welcome," he called back and walked back into the house, chuckling.

"I suppose you heard that?" Silas said into the phone.

"Tell Levi he's my favorite. I'm rebooking your flight right now and will email you your boarding pass. Your flight leaves about twenty minutes after Levi's."

"Got it."

"I'll book you a hotel, too, and a flight to New York tomorrow," she said.

"Thanks, Shannon. Sorry for being a pain in your backside. I'm just trying to not screw this up."

"I know, Si. Good luck today. Call me as soon as the deal is done, and we'll toast over FaceTime."

"You're on."

CHAPTER 27

*L*evi sat on the plane and stared at the empty seat beside him. All those feelings of abandonment came flooding back, and he couldn't help but relive the day two years ago when Silas had stood him up for his career. It was the day that Levi had known it was over. He couldn't trust Silas. He couldn't trust anyone. And he'd called it quits... in an email of all things.

He leaned back against the seat and closed his eyes, trying and failing to block out the intense emotions he couldn't quite shake.

The words of his latest single played in his mind.

Dark days, sleepless nights, struggling to find my way. And then there you were, your name bright in Hollywood lights. You saw me when no one else did. I loved you for you without caring about what you do. Winter nights turned into sunny days. City lights turned to magical fog-soaked bays. If only we'd held on, you'd still be by my side. Instead, I'm here, living in the darkness of my mind.

The song was about love and loss and miscommunication.

But that wasn't what was happening now. They'd just had a

slight change of plans. Silas hadn't stood Levi up. In fact, Levi and Shannon had to work to convince him to go to LA in the first place.

Logically, Levi knew this wasn't remotely the same thing.

But emotionally, seeing that empty seat next to him, his heart and soul felt otherwise.

"Get a grip, Levi," he muttered to himself.

The flight attendant paused at his seat. "Can I get you anything, Mr. Kelley? Water? Juice? A glass of wine?"

"Bloody Mary?" he asked.

"Absolutely." She smiled pleasantly and hurried off to fill his order.

It was still surreal to Levi that he flew first class everywhere he went. As a kid who was kicked out of his house and then used by an uncle to help him do illegal things, Levi never anticipated he'd be anything other than someone who struggled to get by for the rest of his life.

The truth was that Hope and Chad and Silas had been the people who believed in him and made him believe in himself.

And that was just one of the reasons that Levi loved Silas. The feelings of abandonment started to fade. All the rational reasons for him telling Silas to go to LA flooded back, and Levi started to breathe easier.

He glanced at the empty seat beside him again and was relieved when it didn't trigger a response. Leaning back in the seat, he felt his shoulders start to relax.

"Here you go, Mr. Kelley," the flight attendant said, handing him his Bloody Mary. "We'll be taking off shortly, but let me know if you need anything else."

"Thank you." He took a sip of the drink and leaned back into his chair, preparing for the six-hour flight.

The announcement came over the intercom, asking

passengers to turn off their electronics and put their phones into airplane mode. Levi reached for his phone and frowned when he spotted multiple missed calls and a few text messages. All of them were from Candy. He almost clicked off, assuming she wanted to talk about her latest dating angst, but when he spotted Silas's name, he quickly scrolled through the texts.

Levi, call me. It's important! Like now!

Silas can't sign that contract.

It's a trap. The studio is going to tank the project.

Where are you? Call me immediately.

Levi's heart started to race. He had no idea why Candy knew anything about the studio's intentions, but she usually wasn't one to overreact. Even when it came to her dating life, she was more apt to snark about her bad dates and then laugh them off. Her drama was very low-key. He couldn't imagine that she'd text an SOS like this without good reason.

He quickly listened to a couple of voice mails.

Levi, seriously. Where are you? I heard the contract signing is today. Silas cannot go through with it. Stop him. They have no intention of making his show. They just want to tie it up so no one else can. Seriously, I overheard that director guy Marcus talking about it. He tied himself to the project just so he could tank it. Why would he do that? I'm so confused. Call me.

"That bastard!" Levi snarled, remembering the day Marcus had threatened him and Silas if they didn't do the interviews he wanted them to do. Eventually, Levi had told Silas about it, and they'd decided to ignore him. What was he going to do? Sell stories of them to the tabloids? What was one more?

But this? Was Marcus really that petty that he'd kill a project just because he couldn't control Levi and Silas?

Yes. Yes, he was. Levi knew it in his gut.

"Mr. Kelley, I'm going to have to ask you to put your phone in airplane mode," the flight attendant said.

Levi glanced up at her in panic even as he was already calling Silas. "It's an emergency. Just one quick phone call. I swear."

She glanced around with a worried look on her face but then said, "Be very fast. We're getting ready to take off."

He nodded and listened as the phone rang and rang and rang until Silas's voice mail picked up. "Silas. You cannot sign that contract. It's a poison pill. Taking off. Can't explain. Trust me. Don't do anything until we talk again. Please."

Levi ended the call and quickly tapped out a text that said roughly the same thing. Then just as the plane started to speed up and Levi knew he'd done all he could do, he shut down his phone, gripped his drink, and prayed that Silas got his messages.

When the plane was done climbing through the clouds and leveled off, another announcement was made about using electronics. Levi tried to connect to the Wi-Fi but had zero luck. When the attendant came around, she confirmed the Wi-Fi was out. Levi felt sick. He was cut off from the rest of the world until they landed in New York.

On any other day, that would've been just fine with Levi. But this day? He was desperate to have access to at least his text messages, but the universe had other ideas, and he spent the next six hours fidgeting until they landed.

The minute the wheels were down, Levi took his phone out of airplane mode and waited for his texts to update.

Nothing.

No new texts.

He checked his voice mails, but the only one there was from Seth, confirming the venue for the night's concert.

Frantic to find out what happened, Levi tried Silas again. No answer. He texted again, but still no response. In desperation, he tried Shannon, both her mobile number and her landline.

There was no answer from any of them.

He wanted to scream.

Instead, he texted Candy to thank her for the warnings.

Ohmigod, Candy texted back. *Tell me Silas didn't sign that contract.*

I wish I could, but I've been on a plane all day, out of touch, and I have no idea. I'll let you know when I know.

Those bastards deserve butt boils.

He snorted out a tiny laugh and answered, *Butt boils AND puffy skin.*

She sent the crying/laughing emoji.

Once they'd finally deplaned, Levi headed straight for the hotel to check in and drop off his bags. With no word from Silas, he paced his room right up until he had to leave for the concert. Frustrated, he left one more scathing voice mail about returning calls and then yanked the door open.

"Hey," Silas said, grinning at him.

Levi's eyes widened, and his words got caught in his throat as he tried to stammer out a reply.

Silas put his hands on Levi's hips and moved him back into the room. When the door shut softly behind him, he said, "I couldn't wait until tomorrow to see you."

"What happened?" Levi finally demanded, forcing the words out. "And why didn't you call?"

Silas held up his blank phone. "It died. You have the phone chargers."

Levi's heart started to pound against his ribcage as his

223

anxiety ratcheted up to an insane level. "Please tell me you got my messages. You did, right? My text and voice mail?"

"I did." He wrapped his arms around Levi and pulled him in close.

"What did you do? Did you sign the contract?"

"Nope. You told me not to." Silas was staring down at Levi's lips, seeming a lot more interested in kissing him than he was in having this conversation.

But Levi wasn't ready to let it go. "Just like that? I told you not to, and you didn't?"

"Pretty much. The moment I got your message, I canceled the meeting. You wouldn't send me something like that if it was BS, so I called Shannon, had her rebook, and now here I am."

"You don't seem all that upset about it," Levi observed.

"How can I be upset when you saved me from making a giant mistake?"

"Because you were looking forward to this deal. Because we thought you'd actually get to make the series. You lost something important to you today. You're allowed to be upset about that."

Silas nodded, acknowledging Levi's words. "I should be, but do you know what happened right after I canceled the meeting?"

"Are you seriously trying to make me guess?" Levi asked, annoyed at the way this conversation was unfolding.

"Sorry," Silas said with a soft chuckle. "I thought someone would have called you by now. But I guess not. Right after I canceled the meeting, I got a call from Miranda Moon. She said she had a premonition that there were bad actors involved with the deal and if it were her, she wouldn't sign the contract.

When I told her I'd already canceled the meeting, she said something interesting."

Levi sat on the edge of the bed, waiting. "How interesting?"

"She said she's been thinking about opening a production company so that she and Gideon could take on her projects without giving up control. And she's interested in working with me on my series. She said it would be an unusual contract in that I wouldn't get any advance, but I'd have full control and make a better-than-average return on the profit. I told her to sit down with Shannon, work out the details, and I'd think about it."

"You're really interested," Levi said, finally tuning into his energy. He was exuding contentment. Like everything was right in his world.

"More than interested. I know Miranda and Gideon. They are solid people."

"Agreed," Levi said, reaching up and brushing a lock of Silas's hair back behind his ear. "You know, for once I have a gut feeling."

"For once?" Silas said with a disbelieving snort. "You always have gut feelings."

"Okay, true. I think it's more like a vision. Only in my subconscious. Whatever it is, it says Miranda is a good partnership for you."

"I think so, too," Silas said. "Now kiss me. I flew all the way here just to taste those lips."

Levi did as he was asked, but he cut it short and gently pushed Silas back. "We're going to be late."

"For what?" Silas asked.

"My show. I'm debuting my new song tonight, remember?"

"Right. What do you think about debuting something else tonight?"

"Like what? You're not suggesting I moon everyone, are you?" Levi asked, eyeing him with mock suspicion.

"Hardly. That's all for me." Silas ran a hand down the side of Levi's neck, making him shiver. Then he suddenly dropped to one knee and held out a small velvet box.

Levi stared at it, waiting for the panic to set in. The dread that all of this was happening too soon. That they needed more time. But none of those doubts materialized. All he felt was pure happiness. "How long have you been planning this?"

"Does it matter?"

"Maybe." No. No, it didn't. "Ask me anyway."

Silas gave him a knowing smile. "Levi Kelley, I've loved you since I was seventeen. When we were together, when we were apart, and I know for certain I'll love you every day for the rest of my life. Would you please wear my ring and agree to be my husband?"

"Yes." It was as simple as that. No need to justify. Or clarify. Or qualify. Levi loved Silas with his whole heart. He was honored to marry him.

Silas pushed the platinum band with three sparkling diamonds onto Levi's ring finger, and when it was in place, he brought it up to his mouth and kissed it. "I love you, Levi Kelley."

Levi stood, tugging Silas with him, and stepped into his arms. "I love you, too, Silas Ansell."

Levi didn't know who moved first, but suddenly they were kissing. The type of kiss that was full of love and hope and a promise of the future.

Silas pulled back breathlessly and said, "We better get you out of here now, otherwise, I think the only audience you'll have tonight is me and that bed."

Levi shrugged. "Wouldn't bother me."

"*Rolling Stone* might not like it much."

"Fair." Levi reluctantly removed himself from Silas's arms, and together they left so that Levi could put on an iconic show.

The next day, his band's new single rose to the top of the charts in twelve countries. Iconic indeed.

CHAPTER 28

*H*arlow Thane stood behind the counter at Equinox and marveled at the crowd. It was opening night for Chad Garber's new pub, and everyone who was anyone was there, including Silas Ansell and Levi Kelley, the newly engaged couple who were so down to earth it surprised her every time she saw them.

Considering Levi was Chad's brother-in-law, that meant she saw him quite a bit. But his star power still bowled her over.

"Harlow, can I get a soda?" Frankie asked.

"Are you sure that's what you want before you go on stage?" Harlow asked the teenager.

"Ugh. You, too?" she complained. "Now that I'm singing all the time, everyone expects me to just drink water and eat a lot of omega 3s, whatever those are."

"It's good fat to help you sustain energy." Harlow filled up a glass with water and then added a couple of lemon and lime slices for a garnish. "This might help a little."

Frankie took one look at it and grimaced.

"Lemons and limes not your thing?"

"I prefer chocolate."

"Don't we all, kid? Don't we all?"

Frankie took a long sip of her water and then wandered off, leaving it there on Harlow's bar.

She's cute. The voice came out of nowhere, and if Harlow hadn't heard it thousands of times before, it would have startled her.

Harlow ignored the ghost. She didn't have time to play her games. Not today. Not when she was responsible for making sure the opening went off without a hitch.

Sure, Chad was there. But he was busy making the rounds, playing the host. Harlow was the one who was responsible for making sure the event went off without a hitch.

So far so good.

You're going to have to tell them sooner or later, the ghost said right into her ear.

"Go away," Harlow said under her breath. "You're not invited."

The ghost lifted her chin as if she were offended and floated off toward the stage. Harlow eyed her just to make sure she didn't cause any problems, which she was prone to do when she was agitated.

"Hey, Harlow," Miranda Moon said, sliding onto a barstool. "Can I get a vodka and club soda?"

"Sure."

"And a beer for Gideon. Whatever you have on draft that's imported."

Harlow nodded and went to work.

Miranda and her partner had already become frequent visitors of Equinox since they'd rented office space right next door and popped in regularly to see how the renovations were going. They were busy creating a production company, and Harlow had heard the first project they were working on was a television series that Silas Ansell created. It had been big news when they made the announcement. Followed by a scandal with Salish Sea Studios when someone complained about the director of Silas and Levi's movie. Apparently, he'd been sexually harassing a few of the actresses.

There was even talk about shelving the movie, but a fan protest had saved it, citing the fact that none of the actors were involved or knew anything about it, so they shouldn't suffer. It just meant the film wasn't likely to be nominated for anything, but at least the fans would still get to see it.

Harlow handed Miranda her drinks and asked, "Do you want me to put this on a tab?"

"Please." Miranda pulled out her credit card and handed it over. "I think we're gonna be here a while."

"Chad will be pleased to hear it," Harlow joked.

"So is that ghost that's ogling my Gideon," Miranda said.

Harlow knew exactly who she was talking about but didn't turn in the ghost's direction. That would be a dead giveaway that she was a medium, and that was something Harlow intentionally left behind many months ago. "Yeah? Is she cute, or does she have a wart on her nose?"

Miranda rolled her eyes. "Don't play that game with me, Harlow. I know you see her. I know you've tried to eradicate her from the pub, but can't because she's rooted here. What I don't understand is why you act like you don't know."

"It's complicated," Harlow said, deciding to just own her gift or curse or whatever anyone wanted to call it.

"It always is, dear." Miranda patted her hand. "If you ever want help or need to talk, I'm here."

"Thank you," Harlow said. "But I'm out of the ghost business."

"That's hard to believe," a deep, lyrical voice said. A voice she'd never forgotten.

Harlow spun around and stared straight into the eyes of her old partner.

Cash Moses.

Her ex-best friend. Ex-partner. Ex-lover.

He was the last person she'd expected to see in Keating Hollow.

"Cash? What the hell are you doing here?"

"The same thing you are," he said with a wry smile as he looked her up and down. "Looking for that ghost who stole everything from us."

"A ghost and a betrayal? Oh, this is going to be good," Miranda said, rubbing her hands together in gleeful anticipation.

Cash glanced at the novelist turned producer. "You're damned right it is. Harlow, are you ready for this?"

No. He was talking about hunting the one ghost who she'd never been able to communicate with. The one who'd stolen priceless family antiques and jewelry pieces and had ruined Harlow's television career. While Harlow wanted desperately to end the spirit, she most definitely was not ready for a battle. Not yet. And not when it involved Cash Moses. But she'd never admit that. Instead, she gave him a cheeky grin and said, "Bring it on."

CHAPTER 29

*A*ugust West hauled the paddleboard off the top of his SUV and made his way down to the water's edge where Silas and Levi were waiting for him, both dressed in wetsuits and looking a little miserable about being up so early. They never did get a day to paddleboard when he'd been in Keating Hollow working on their movie. The photographers had just been too relentless. But now that they were in Befana Bay, they were protected from the paparazzi and August was determined to show them a good time.

It was just before sunrise and there was a pretty good chill in the air, but there was no wind and Befana Bay was as crystal clear and calm as could be. It was the perfect morning for paddleboarding.

"You two are in for a treat," August said. "Perfect conditions."

"That's what I told Levi, but he's still not convinced," Silas said, smirking at his fiancé.

"Listen, I said it was beautiful, but I'm not sure why we have to be out here so early," Levi said with a groan. "This is supposed to be a vacation before you start work on your series and I go out on tour."

"Trust me," August said. "It'll be worth it. I have a surprise for you guys."

"I hope it involves pastries," Levi quipped.

"Mmm, pastries. And cappuccinos," Silas added.

August shook his head and couldn't stop the laugh that bubbled out of his throat. "You two are like teenagers with no impulse control. I swear, you were made for each other."

"Thanks. We think so, too," Silas said, grinning from ear to ear.

"Yep," Levi agreed, staring at his man with adoration.

It really was heartwarming to see how much the two men cared for each other. August hadn't ever been that in love. In lust maybe, but not love. He was starting to wonder if it was even in his DNA to date and settle down with one person.

He doubted it, but he remained open.

"All right then, ready?" August asked as he floated his board.

"Ready," they said together.

He took his time going over all the safety procedures, how to stand and balance, what to do if they fell off, and then lastly, how to behave if any sea life emerged or approached them.

"So you're saying that if a whale surfaces, we're just supposed to do nothing? Just stand there and let it do its thing?" Levi asked, sounding horrified.

August chuckled. "Yes. That's exactly right. Orcas aren't aggressive to humans. If they show up, just stand there on your board and watch them. I promise you, it's magical."

"Do you know what they call orcas? Killer whales. I think they call them that for a reason, August," Levi countered.

"You'll be fine," August assured him. "Never had an issue with orcas or killer whales."

"I'll protect you, babe," Silas said as he held Levi's board to help him kneel on it.

"That's why I love you." Levi blew him a kiss.

August stood back and watched them, both jealous and nauseated. Okay, maybe just jealous, but he thought he *should* be nauseated. His friends were not shy about the PDA.

It didn't take either of them long to get used to the paddleboards and even less time to learn to stand.

August cheered them on and then eventually joined them on his own board. He paddled out a fair distance into the bay, waving for Silas and Levi to follow him. Then he heard it. The unmistakable call of the orcas.

"They're coming," August whispered.

"Who is?" Silas asked.

"The orcas. Just wait."

As the moment ticked by, suddenly the bay was flooded with witches on their own paddleboards. They were dressed in black robes and pointy black witch's hats, and each one of them carried a lit candle in one hand. The effect was a gorgeous glow over the darkened waters.

"Wow," Levi breathed from a space just to the left of August. Silas was on the other side, making them form sort of a triangle.

August chuckled to himself about how the tabloids might spin this if they saw it. Luckily, they couldn't penetrate the magical wards that surrounded Befana Bay. Those wards were why so many A-list actors were willing to film in the town. It was always about the privacy.

"Look," August told them, nodding toward the opening of the bay. "They're coming."

With the moon still shining silver on the bay, August watched as a pod of twenty orcas circled them and the coven who'd come to talk to the orcas. Levi and Silas were struck speechless by the experience.

The leader of the coven spoke in a language that mirrored that of the orcas, and they all spoke back as they skimmed through the water, delighting them with their beauty. There were never any words that could express the magical experience that happened when the orcas arrived. And August didn't even want to try. He just soaked it in. And when the orcas disappeared, he felt like he'd been touched by nature.

"August," Silas breathed as he glided closer. "Why haven't we done that before?"

"I don't know," he admitted. "It didn't feel right at the time. I think you were meant to experience that with Levi." His gut told him that was the truth. August had a knack for knowing what other people needed during different stages of their lives.

"You know, I think you're right."

The three men paddled back to shore and watched the coven, who'd stayed out in the bay conducting their ritualistic chants and practicing their spells. There were flashes of light here and there, but as soon as the sun started to rise, they immediately headed back in.

"I think I need a drink after that," Levi said. "I can't get over it. Thanks, August. I don't think that's something I'll ever forget."

"You're welcome. If you want another adventure while you're here, we can visit Cassandra, the fortune teller. She's always a crowd favorite with her tarot readings."

"I'll pass," Silas said. "I think I'd rather go kayaking or hiking."

"I'm down," Levi told August. "We can go while Silas is napping. He's an old man now who likes a nap every day."

"Hey. I'm not even pushing thirty yet. That's not old. I'm

just catching up on all that sleep I missed when I was working so much before," Silas insisted.

"You get no pushback from me," August said. "Naps will keep you rested and young."

Levi promised to text August later to plan a trip to Cassandra's and then the couple took off for the local coffee shop, leaving August to deal with the paddleboards. He didn't mind. He didn't have much else to do that day. At least not yet anyway. He was between jobs at the moment and usually spent his days assisting whoever needed help around town. Sometimes that was mowing yards. Other days it might be jumpstarting a car. And then other people required more specialized help.

Like Sage Easton.

Every time he ran into her, he had the sense that she needed him. Only he wasn't exactly sure for what. And today was no exception.

He knew she was in the parking lot even before he spotted her red Toyota Rav4. He always knew when Sage was around. It was her intense energy.

Sage was a very driven woman. She worked hard, which he respected, but that's all she really did. Work. All the time. And visit her grandmother, whose house was at the other end of the parking lot.

Because he loved Bethany Befana and he could never get enough of Sage West, he strolled over to the house and leaned against the front gate, watching as the two women spoke on the porch. They looked to be having an intense conversation, and he didn't want to interrupt.

But then suddenly, there was a loud crack and a flash of light that left Sage standing stock-still and speechless.

"There. It's done," Bethany declared. "No witch was made

DEANNA CHASE

to spend every single day working. Now you'll *have* to figure out how to have fun. Don't come back here until you do." The older woman gave August a nod, indicating she'd seen him, and then with her head held high, she walked back into her house.

Sage stared dumbly at the closed door. Finally, she seemed to come back to herself and stalked off the porch, anger radiating from her like a fireball.

"Are you all right?" August asked her when she reached him.

Sage glared at him. "No."

He raised his eyebrows. "Did your grandmother just do what I think she did?"

"If you mean strip my magic, then yes. Yes, she did. Can you believe her? The audacity. She thinks I don't know how to have fun."

"Do you?" August asked, suspecting that Bethany would have never done something so drastic otherwise.

"I have fun!" she cried, balling her fists up in frustration.

"Nah, I think your grandmother is right. You need lessons in fun," he said, giving her an easy smile.

"Oh? And you think you're the man to do it?" she shot back.

"Yep. I'm exactly who you need," he said, knowing he sounded like an arrogant SOB. But he couldn't help it if he was confident. August West was a master of fun.

She scoffed. "Forget it. I'd rather hire crotchety old man Peter White than deal with"—she waved a hand up and down as she took in his disheveled appearance—"whatever this is."

He watched her stalk up the street toward her glass shop, knowing she wouldn't be able to make any new product until she got her magic back. "I'll be here when you're ready," he called after her.

When all she did was raise one hand and flip him off, he threw back his head and laughed, knowing without a doubt that she'd be at his doorstep to hire him as her fun couch within the week.

And he was going to enjoy the hell out of every minute of it.

DEANNA'S BOOK LIST

Witches of Keating Hollow:
Soul of the Witch
Heart of the Witch
Spirit of the Witch
Dreams of the Witch
Courage of the Witch
Love of the Witch
Power of the Witch
Essence of the Witch
Muse of the Witch
Vision of the Witch
Waking of the Witch
Honor of the Witch
Promise of the Witch
Return of the Witch
Fortune of the Witch

Witches of Befana Bay:
The Witch's Silver Lining

Witches of Christmas Grove:
A Witch For Mr. Holiday
A Witch For Mr. Christmas
A Witch For Mr. Winter
A Witch For Mr. Mistletoe
A Witch For Mr. Frost

Premonition Pointe Novels:
Witching For Grace
Witching For Hope
Witching For Joy
Witching For Clarity
Witching For Moxie
Witching For Kismet

Miss Matched Midlife Dating Agency:
Star-crossed Witch
Honor-bound Witch
Outmatched Witch
Moonstruck Witch

Jade Calhoun Novels:
Haunted on Bourbon Street
Witches of Bourbon Street
Demons of Bourbon Street
Angels of Bourbon Street
Shadows of Bourbon Street
Incubus of Bourbon Street
Bewitched on Bourbon Street
Hexed on Bourbon Street
Dragons of Bourbon Street

Pyper Rayne Novels:
Spirits, Stilettos, and a Silver Bustier
Spirits, Rock Stars, and a Midnight Chocolate Bar
Spirits, Beignets, and a Bayou Biker Gang
Spirits, Diamonds, and a Drive-thru Daiquiri Stand
Spirits, Spells, and Wedding Bells

Ida May Chronicles:
Witched To Death
Witch, Please
Stop Your Witchin'

Crescent City Fae Novels:
Influential Magic
Irresistible Magic
Intoxicating Magic

Last Witch Standing:
Bewitched by Moonlight
Soulless at Sunset
Bloodlust By Midnight
Bitten At Daybreak

Witch Island Brides:
The Wolf's New Year Bride
The Vampire's Last Dance
The Warlock's Enchanted Kiss
The Shifter's First Bite

Destiny Novels:
Defining Destiny
Accepting Fate

Wolves of the Rising Sun:

Jace

Aiden

Luc

Craved

Silas

Darien

Wren

Black Bear Outlaws:

Cyrus

Chase

Cole

Bayou Springs Alien Mail Order Brides:

Zeke

Gunn

Echo

ABOUT THE AUTHOR

New York Times and USA Today bestselling author, Deanna Chase, is a native Californian, transplanted to the slower paced lifestyle of southeastern Louisiana. When she isn't writing, she is often goofing off with her husband in New Orleans or playing with her two shih tzu dogs. For more information and updates on newest releases visit her website at deannachase.com.

Made in the USA
Las Vegas, NV
11 June 2023

73276059R00146